Average Joe

John L. Davis IV

DEDICATION

For Astrid and Hannah, the best daughters an average dad could ever want.

Average Joe

Chapter 1

It was a normal work day for Joe Pruitt until he saw the teenage girl yanked into a white van only a few feet away.

He had just finished setting a new windshield into a Prius and was standing at the open door of his Fast Glass work truck. He'd stripped off his gloves, tossed them in the seat and picked up the clip-board waiting there. Then, he fumbled his pen, dropping it, where it rolled beneath the vehicle.

Stooping down on hands and knees with his arm reaching under the truck, he glanced to the side when he heard tires screech to a halt. He assumed someone had probably come close to running the stoplight. Instead, he saw a long white van in pristine condition skid to a stop next to a girl that looked to be thirteen or fourteen years old. She was wearing earbuds, bopping along to the beat of some tune that he would probably despise, her backpack bouncing on her shoulder. She wore blue denim shorts and a pink t-shirt that said SWEET across the front in slanted script.

The girl had apparently heard the squeal of the tires as well, or maybe caught sight of the van out of the corner of her eye. She looked up from her phone just as the door slid open and a man with a thin brown beard and thick forearms leaned out, grabbed the girl by an arm and violently jerked her into the vehicle. Her head snapped to the side as her backpack slid off her shoulder and thumped to the ground. It happened so fast. As she disappeared into the dark maw of the wide door, she never made a sound, had no chance to even cry out.

Joe took no time to think before he reacted. If he had taken even seconds to consider what he was about to do, the van, and the girl inside would have been gone.

Jumping up just as the sliding door slammed shut, Joe charged toward the van, legs pumping high and hard to cross three empty parking spaces and the sidewalk between his own vehicle and the kidnappers'.

If the light had been green or if there hadn't been a car and a lumbering tow truck passing through the intersection, he would have been too late, no matter how hard he ran.

When the van was forced to slow to let the other vehicles cross, Joe, without a plan or thought to what came next, jumped up onto the narrow wire-mesh foot-board, wrapped his fingers around a three-rung ladder mounted to the back door, and held on as the van's tires screeched on pavement and tore through the intersection.

Chapter 2

The day had begun like every other day for Joe Pruitt with his alarm clock at 5:30, sitting at the little kitchen table with his first cup of coffee and then half-an-hour in the bathroom reading news on his cell phone while taking care of business. He ate a quick breakfast of toast and a fried egg with a couple pieces of microwave sausage as he checked his email to see what his daily assignments were, then, he took a shower.

With his travel cup filled and the coffeepot off (he always checked it twice to be sure), Joe would get into his beater pickup and head to the yard to get his work truck, load up with any glass he would need for installations, check in at the office and he was on the road for the rest of the day.

The job had a one-hundred-mile radius and being in the Missouri Bootheel meant that he would get calls for Illinois, Kentucky, Tennessee, and Arkansas, with the rare auto-glass repair or replacement in the north-western corner of Mississippi.

He had started out the day with a windshield replacement outside Poplar Bluff, Missouri. He was then called for two chip repairs; one in Doniphan, and the next in Corning, Arkansas; followed by another replacement in Walnut Ridge. He had just been finishing up when the call came in for an emergency replacement in Jonesboro, Arkansas.

A Prius windshield that had been smashed by a baseball bat when a disgruntled ex-employee decided to exact revenge on her former employer.

Joe could track every single moment of the day that now led to him clinging to the back of a kidnapper's van, hurtling down a side street in Jonesboro, Arkansas. What he couldn't track was his own thinking. How he allowed himself to be in this position. Why hadn't he just called the cops or followed them in his own truck.

Jumping onto the vehicle had been an impulse, and one that he himself couldn't comprehend. He was no hero. He had no military training, he wasn't a former police officer. He wasn't an award-winning martial arts champion, nor was he someone who carried a gun everywhere he went.

Joe Pruitt was just an average guy who went to work, paid his child-support on time, and often fell asleep at night on the couch with Netflix playing episode after episode of a show he wasn't really watching.

Now, he was latched onto the back of a moving vehicle, hanging on for all he was worth in an effort to what, rescue a kidnapped girl he didn't know?

"Jesus, Joe, what the hell are you doing?" he muttered. The sound was snatched away by the rushing wind.

Chapter 3

From inside the van, Joe heard a shout and pressed his ear against the glass, which appeared to have been painted or blacked out on the interior because no light shone through. He could only see his own reflection, grim and tight, staring back at him.

Another shout, this one much clearer, then what sounded to him like dropping a package of meat on a countertop, followed by a girlish scream, high and painful even through the glass. Someone was getting slapped.

Joe cringed at the sound.

"Stop hitting her, damn it! Boss man's gonna be pissed if you mess up the merchandise!"

Merchandise? Joe thought.

"The little bitch damn near bit my thumb off!"

Joe felt a grin tug at the corners of his mouth. You go girl, he thought.

"Serves you right for trying to feel 'er up. Get the cuffs on her, hit her with the chloroform and leave her the hell alone. How many times you have to be told this shit, man?"

"Screw you! It's stupid we can't have a little fun with 'em."

"Yeah, well, the buyers like their purchases to be blemish free and unused whenever possible, so hands off."

Joe's stomach sank when he realized the two

men were talking about human trafficking. They were taking this girl to someone, and she would be sold off, probably to the highest bidder like cattle at an auction. For a moment, he felt as if he were going to vomit. Then he did, and for several seconds it looked like the van had a bad case of diarrhea, leaving a reeking trail of mess behind it.

He took his right hand off the ladder rung and wiped it across his mouth, then dropped it to scrub the sour-tasting spittle onto his pant-leg. The back of his hand bumped his cell phone, which was still clipped to his belt.

Cell-phone! Holy shit, man, start using your brain, he thought. Cautiously, he popped the phone free of its clip-on case, and with one hand tucked tightly behind the ladder rung, he used both hands to grip it and unlock the screen. Carefully, he swiped to bring up the dial pad, and punched in 9-1-1.

"Nine-one-one, what's the nature of your emergency?"

As softly as he possibly could, Joe said, "I've seen a kidnapping!"

"I'm sorry sir, but it's very difficult to hear you. Did you say you've been kidnapped?"

"No, I saw one! I'm hanging on the back of their van! They don't..."

The van swerved to miss a pothole, throwing Joe off balance. His wrist, which was still wedged between the door and the ladder rung, felt as if it were going to snap. He yanked it free, reaching for the ladder with the hand currently holding the phone.

The phone hit the ladder, popped free of his grip, and sailed through the air. It arced up and out, behind the van, and Joe watched in shock as the device hit the blacktop, bounced once and broke apart, its pieces tumbling to rest in the middle of the road.

His shoulders sagged, and his head dropped, his one lifeline and possibly the only way to help himself and the girl in the van now lay in the middle of the street far behind him, in pieces.

He was surprised to see another phone sail by and shatter on the pavement moments later. Then it dawned on him. The girl's phone.

Chapter 4

The road continued to peel away from under the car, passing between his feet as he watched, still stunned over the loss of his phone. The van turned once, and then again, a mile later then changed direction once more two miles after that. Heading deeper into the rural areas, he considered jumping off at each turn, but was certain that he would break an ankle, the driver would see him, or both.

Neither option was ideal, but the thought of the driver seeing him and possibly pulling over long enough to put a bullet in his head, kept him on the back of the van.

Once he had calmed his frantic thoughts, Joe was able to consider his situation. He wondered if anyone else at the intersection had seen the girl get snatched into the van, or if they had witnessed him jumping onto the back and hanging on.

How, in the modern world where everyone seemed to have a camera ready for even the most mundane of incidents, could no one have seen anything. How, in a town with over 70,000 residents could a child get kidnapped in broad daylight without someone other than himself seeing it, especially outside a business that sat right on a busy intersection.

He was baffled by the concept, that this could happen. He would have thought it the plot of a thriller movie, possibly something starring

Halle Berry, if he wasn't actually clinging to the back of the kidnapper's van at that very moment.

Now the town was far behind him, and somehow there had been no other traffic. It was as if some wicked supernatural force were keeping other drivers at bay, so that evil deeds would go unseen. Joe kept watching, hoping that a car would suddenly turn off a side road behind them. Someone he could wave down and signal to call the cops.

Joe shuffled his feet on the foot board, settling in. Gently, he rested his head against the cool metal of the ladder and closed his eyes for a moment. Sucking in several deep breaths and releasing them slowly he muttered, "Figure it out, Joe. Figure it out."

He felt the van slow as it turned right, the road becoming rough. He opened his eyes to see gravel instead of blacktop. They were far out into the country now.

He almost let go of the ladder when a horn wailed behind him, several long blasts. A car!

He turned to see a rust-eaten pickup truck turning onto the road the van had just left. The driver was hanging out the window, waving at him, shouting "Woooo ride it, buddy!" as he blasted the horn again.

Joe waved wildly with one arm, and mimicked holding a phone to his ear, but the distance by that point was too great, and the truck had left the gravel for the blacktop and was gone with a squeal of tires and another wild shout.

From inside the van Joe heard, "What the hell was that?"

"Some country-boy asshole. How should I know? Probably on the way to pick up his sister for a hot date."

"Ha! Yeah, probably. A little seester-wyyyfe luuuvin'," the voice drawled, chuckling. "Fuckin' hillbillies."

It sounded like both men were now sitting toward the front of the van.

Joe wanted to scream his frustration, to punch the door of the van in anger. He only sagged against it and clenched the hand not holding the ladder in a tight ball of rage.

Chapter 5

Dust from the gravel road created a thick plume behind the van, and Joe had to tug his shirt up over his mouth to keep from inhaling it. Still, he was forced to take shallow breaths because of the bitter grit.

It was a long twenty minutes before the van slowed again, and Joe had begun to think that he would pass out from oxygen deprivation before he was able to get another full breath of fresh air.

He could see himself keeling over unconscious, falling from the back of the van and tumbling along the gravel road, his skin being peeled away by the rock. Maybe if he was lucky, he'd bust his head and never wake up again. No pain. No more white van. No more kidnapped girl.

The kidnapped girl!

He had yet to come up with something to help her, or himself. Maybe just hanging on and finding out where they were taking the girl, then going for help would be her best chance. However: he would have to get off the van and hide before they saw him.

The van slowed again, making a left turn. A wide-open field swept away behind him, and suddenly they were on a dirt track with trees on both sides. The further they drove, the denser the trees became.

We're way the hell out in the middle of nowhere, aren't we, Joe thought, while noticing that going for help just got a lot more difficult.

The van slowed, and a voice shouted, "Where the hell have you two been!?"

The van stopped abruptly, slamming Joe's face into the ladder.

Joe's heart began to pound when he heard the front doors open and feet drop out to the ground.

"Don't worry about it. We got the merchandise, two of 'em actually. Saw an opportunity and took it. Where's the boss?"

"You snatched another one? What the hell were you two dumbasses thinking? What if someone had seen you?"

"Shit man, nobody sees anything anymore. She was just walking, we grabbed her and were gone. It's all good. And she's a sweet one too, worth at least ten grand, easy."

Joe's mind raced with too many thoughts. Two girls. One had already been in the van when they grabbed the girl off the street. They had been sent after the first one, so they were targeting specific girls. Why specific ones? And where was he going to hide?

"Get them unloaded and in the house with the others. You can talk to the boss after that. Looks like we're going to be out here a few more days before the hand-off."

"Oh come on! I hate this country bullshit!"

Joe's eyes grew wide. Others in the house? One thought kept repeating in his mind, even as he was considering how to hide as the men talked. What the hell have you gotten into, Joe?

Booted feet shifted on the dirt. The van door slid open. "The other girl's all the way at the back."

"Fine, I'll get 'er."

Joe swore silently and glanced down at his feet. He was only seconds from being discovered and he knew one thing for sure. When they caught him, he was dead.

Chapter 6

"What the hell!?"

"What the hell, what?"

"It looks like somebody puked on the van. Come 'ere and look at this."

"I don't wanna see somebody else's puke."

"Well, who the hell did it? It's on the door, and the step."

"How should I know? Just get the girl and come on."

Joe watched as booted feet stopped inches from his face. He heard the rear doors open and the man grunt like he was lifting something heavy.

"This one's a little on the chunky side." The booted feet turned and moved away.

"That's what the guy ordered."

The chattering voices of the men from the van dwindled, and Joe dropped his face into the dirt underneath the van, puffing out the breath he'd been holding. "Son-of-a-bitch," he whispered into the grit.

He was thankful that the van sat high off the ground; otherwise, he never would have been able to slip underneath as quickly has he had. Being a few inches under six feet tall had its advantages, as did the fact that he had gone from two-hundred forty-five pounds to just over two-hundred after Anne left him. It was the only good thing about the whiskey diet he'd been on for almost three months after the divorce.

Slowly, limiting the noise, Joe turned so that he faced the opposite direction. He could see the kidnapper's feet as they reached the house and went up the worn front steps of a farmhouse that, while not abandoned, looked as if it hadn't been properly cared for in years.

His narrow view showed him little beyond the porch and he didn't want to slide forward to get a better look, preferring to stay in the deep shadow beneath the vehicle for the time being.

He dropped his face to the dirt and closed his eyes for a moment, letting his heart slow its rapid pace. Even as his heartbeat slowed, Joe's mind raced. There were too many thoughts to catch one before another took its place, all of them frantic and disjointed.

Thoughts of his ex-wife, and his daughter Cady Lynn invaded his mind. How he missed seeing her, even when it was only on weekends. Since Anne had remarried and moved to California with her new husband, he'd only seen Cady Lynn once.

Now, inside the house before him, were two girls whose families may already be missing them. Two girls who might not even fully understand what was happening or what would happen to them once these men sold them off, and here he was, stuck beneath a kidnapper's van, almost too terrified to move. Certain that the moment he crawled from underneath and tried to run, he would be spotted and gunned down.

This was a job for the police or the FBI. It was a task for an action hero. If this were a movie, he thought, he would be someone huge, like Dwayne Johnson, and he would have already killed or beaten most of the kidnappers and carried the two girls to safety on his massive shoulders. Except, this was no movie and he was no hero. The one thought that kept pressing in among all the others was "I'm just a guy, I shouldn't be here."

Chapter 7

Joe waited beneath the van for what felt like hours, but without his phone to check the time, he had no way of knowing how long it had been. He had stopped wearing a watch ages ago, soon after getting his first mobile phone. The light beyond the van's bumper hadn't changed much, so it couldn't have been nearly as long as it felt.

He crawled forward, scraping over the dirt, until his head was at the line where shadow and light met, just under the front bumper. The heat from the engine and the dark, cloying odor of burnt oil seemed to press on him as if the air had been let out of the tires, allowing the van to settle onto his back. He closed his eyes and took shallow breaths, fighting a momentary bout of claustrophobia. Once his head had cleared, Joe was able to focus once more on the trouble in front of him.

His initial assessment of the house had been spot-on. It was time-worn and run down, much of the paint on the old siding had chipped away or faded, several broken windows had been covered in tape and plastic, and the roof on the western corner sagged. Lights could be seen in two windows, so the place had power.

Joe watched for close to ten minutes. He saw a shadowed form pass in front of a light in a window, and nothing more for a while. He worked several plans over in his mind while watching, each of them usually ending in him getting shot. None of them with the kids getting rescued.

Joe jerked and bumped his head when the front door came open and one of the men stepped out onto the porch. He was tall, over six feet, with black hair past his ears. A glint of light reflected from what Joe assumed was a lip piercing, though he couldn't see it from this far away.

His heavy steps pounded on weathered boards, and for a moment, Joe prayed they would crack beneath him and drop the man to ground, breaking his ankle or spearing him in the crotch with a jagged sliver of wood.

Joe scrambled backward, just enough to stay out of sight. The man stopped at the edge of the porch, unzipped his fly and proceeded to urinate into the dry grass beyond, shaking his hips so that his piss made wide streamers.

When he was done, he zipped up and turned back toward the front door. Joe cringed when he stopped and glared at the van. Toward the house he shouted, "Hey, Mike, you left the back door open on the van, asshole!"

A muffled shout from inside the house. "Well, go close it!"

"Screw you, dude. You close it, I'm not your bitch."

"I'll get it later. I'm busy!"

"Doing what, pullin' yer tiny dick?!"

"Piss off!"

The man with the piercing laughed, shook his head and walked back into the house.

Joe slid backwards even further. The back of the van was open. Maybe they left the keys, or there was a gun inside. Anything that might help him reach the authorities, rescue the girls, or at least get away.

He hadn't seen another vehicle. Either it was out of sight behind the house, or they had all come in this one van.

He could slide out and slip into the van unseen by anyone in the house.

Chapter 8

Joe didn't bother to brush away the dirt covering his front. He slid all the way out from the van and cast a quick glance around before lifting his head far enough to peer inside. It was too dark to see much of anything other than some rags, and a few drops of blood.

Pushing aside his apprehension, Joe climbed in and stayed low, on his hands and knees. As he crawled toward the front seats, he avoided several more drops of blood, a torn t-shirt, and a backpack, it's contents of textbooks and notebooks spilling from the ripped open top. There was nothing else in the back of the van.

Keeping his head down, Joe felt between the seats, hoping to find a gun, something, anything, to defend himself with. In front of his face was a console with a flip up top. He reached forward and pressed a button. The flap sprang up, but Joe was disappointed to find nothing more than some napkins, and several packets of ketchup.

It seemed unreal to him, that these people would eat the same fast food as much of America. As if they would somehow subsist on fear and pain and the misery of tortured youth instead of Big Macs and fries with ketchup.

He reached over the passenger seat and popped open the wide glove compartment. Again, nothing but some papers, the owner's manual, a granola bar, and a tiny plastic box of fuses. He kept the granola bar.

As he was leaning back he caught a faint

twinkle of light from the passenger seat. On the seat, face down, its black case blending almost perfectly with the black seat, lay a cell phone. The twinkle had come from light reflected off the small circle of the camera lens.

"Oh shit," he said. Though he only whispered it, he peeked above the dash, toward the house. No one was coming.

Grabbing the phone, Joe scooted backward, no longer paying attention to the spots of blood. Kneeling in the middle of the floor, he held the phone in front of him like a sacred object. "Please don't be password locked." His heart was already beginning to hammer in his chest as he pressed the button on the side to bring the screen to life.

The screen lit up to show him a pattern of dots. His wife had used the same type of lockout on her phone.

"Son of a bitch!" He spat. Part of him wanted to snap the phone in half, to crush it in his bare hands and he squeezed it tightly for several slamming heartbeats before he realized that on the screen, below the lock grid was an icon that said *Emergency*.

His fingers shook as he tapped it and a dial-pad came up. "Oh God…" He punched in 9-1-1, lifted the phone to his ear and almost cried out when a voice came on the other end and said, "Nine-one-one, what is the nature of your emergency?"

Chapter 9

"I've witnessed a kidnapping!" Joe had to work to keep his voice low and calm and not spit everything out in a rush of overexcited nerves.

"You've witnessed a kidnapping, sir?"

"Yes, I'm hiding outside the house right now, in the back of the van they used to kidnap two girls."

"Ok, sir. Can you give me your name?"

"Joe... Joe Pruitt."

"Ok, Joe, you said you're outside their house right now? Can you tell me where that's located?"

"I have no clue where I'm at. I saw them grab this girl, and I jumped on the van. I don't know why, I just did. It was the only thing I could think of to do. They haven't seen me. They drove for a long time after they grabbed her. I was hanging on the van, on the back, and..."

The words began to spill free and, for a moment, Joe lost himself to the intensity of it all. Tears welled in his eyes, his heart hammered wildly in his chest, his palms grew slick, and he struggled to draw a deep breath.

"Mr. Pruitt... Joe, take a breath, you're doing fine. I understand this has all been very stressful. I've notified the county police, and they're going to start searching the area. Can you tell me anything about your location?"

"Uh, the house looks like it hasn't been lived in for a long time, but there's power on, I can see lights inside. It's white or used to be. A lot of the paint has chipped off or faded, now it looks kind of gray. Some of the windows have plastic on them."

"Can you see any landmarks from your location? A barn or shed, another house or route number? Anything at all?"

The woman's calm, easy voice helped him focus. "Let me look." Keeping the phone to his ear he raised up, slowly widening the sliver of windshield and everything beyond it.

Angling his head, and looking to the left of the van, away from the trees to his right, Joe could see a barn or large shed, half caved in. "Yeah, there's a barn, uh, brown, old, half of it's caved in on the left side. The yard has some old, rusted farm stuff just sitting around. I don't see any numbers."

The woman's smooth voice said, "Ok, Joe, that's great, perfect. Now, you say you're hiding inside the kidnapper's van, correct?"

"Yes."

"You may want to look for a better place to hide until the police arrive, Joe. Is there anywhere nearby? Can you get to that barn?"

The idea of charging across the wide-open overgrown yard to the barn caused a pit to form in Joe's gut. "No, I'd be in full view of the house. There's a bunch of trees right next to the van, like a few feet away. I might be able to get there without being seen."

"Ok, good. Joe, keep the phone on and with you and do just that."

"Ok, I'll let you know when I'm there."

Lowering the phone, Joe glanced up over the dash once more, sucked in a deep breath and scooted to the open rear door. He looked out, slid legs first until his feet touched the ground, and stood, his knees shaky.

Joe side-stepped to the edge of the door, peeked around, and took another breath. Just go, he thought, just go. He went.

The stretch of trees was thick with overgrowth and about fifteen feet from where the van sat in the dirt drive if he ran a straight line from the vehicle to woods. Instead, he angled back along the dirt driveway, keeping the van between himself and the house for as long as possible before making for the tree-line.

Joe crouched into an awkward run, hit the edge of the trees and dove over a tangle of vines and overgrowth. The dark blue Fast Glass jacket he wore tore on the side where it caught a branch, and something jabbed deep into his left hand when he hit the ground. The phone, in his right hand, was safe.

He lay there, unmoving for a count of ten, listening for shouts from the house, almost certain that he had been seen. When the drumming of the blood in his ears slowed and he heard nothing from the house, Joe pressed the phone to his ear and said softly, "I'm in the woods. I don't think they saw me. I'm gonna move a little deeper."

"Ok, Joe, good."

Joe pushed fifteen yards into the heavy

underbrush, wincing at every sound. He stopped and crouched next to an old oak wide enough to hide behind. Lifting the phone again, he said, "Ok, I think I'm hidden pretty good."

"Ok, Joe, that's great. You stay there, and we should have an officer out soon."

"There are at least three guys, maybe more."

"I'll let the officers know."

A tone sounded in Joe's ear and he pulled the phone away from his face to look at the screen. "Crap." Speaking to the dispatcher he said, "The battery's getting low. I'm gonna hang up just in case I need to call again."

"Ok, Joe. Just stay where you are and wait for the officers to secure the location when they arrive."

"Ok, can do, and thanks."

"You're welcome, Mr. Pruitt."

Joe tapped the end button, stuffed the phone into his jacket pocket, and hunkered down next to the tree. From his position, he could see glimpses of the house, including the front door, and the van.

He took a deep breath and sagged against the tree. His heartbeat began to slow, enough so that he didn't feel as if he were going to have the heart attack his doctor had cautioned him would come if he didn't start exercising and eating better. Heart's getting plenty of exercise today, he thought. Knowing the cops were on the way, he allowed himself to relax, sit down and stretch out his legs beside the tree.

Don't get too comfortable, you're not out of

the woods yet. A faint smiled creased his face at the joke.

Then the thing he feared the most happened.

Through the woods he heard the front door of the house slam open and a voice shout "Find him!"

Chapter 10

Four guys, one of them the porch-pisser, stormed out of the house. One man, Joe was unable to make out anything about him, stood on the porch while the other three charged down the steps while the one left on the porch shouted orders.

"Mike, check the van! Dave, that old fucking barn! Evan, look around the house. Find this guy!"

Just as Joe began to process the question of how the men knew he was out there, he heard a car, then saw flashing red and blue lights through the trees.

Oh, thank God! He thought. He wanted to shout, "You bastards are in the shit now!" Instead, he stayed low next to the tree and watched. Part of him hoped there wasn't a gunfight between the police and the kidnappers. The rest of him hoped the cops shot them all.

Daylight was beginning to fade as the police car pulled into the drive. Joe caught glimpses of it through the trees. When the car stopped, he was able to angle his head enough to get a decent view of the officer when he stepped out with his pistol drawn.

A shout from the house. The man issuing orders yelled, "Hello, officer!"

"Don't you 'Hello, officer' me!"

Joe kept his emotions tamped down, despite the running thought of *Get 'em, get 'em*!

The cop took several steps forward, standing now just behind the white van. "What the hell's going on out here, Peavey! I get a call from dispatch about some guy who's witnessed a kidnapping, he described this place perfectly."

Joe looked back toward the house. The man who had been issuing orders walked down the steps, disappearing and reappearing like some evil wraith as the trees interrupted Joe's view. Joe was concerned about the searchers, but he had lost sight of all three men. Why hadn't they come running when the cop showed up?

"I want an extra five grand for this, Peavey! I'm gonna have to spin a yarn to dispatch about finding some weirdo in his car with his dick in his hand, getting off on sending cops on a wild goose chase. We can't have this shit!"

The man from the porch now stood in front of the cop and Joe had to strain to hear their voices. He wasn't about to attempt moving closer.

"I'll give you three thousand, just for the trouble, Sheriff, but don't think you can fleece me. It won't end well. We didn't know anything about this guy until you called."

Joe's heart sank into his stomach, which churned unpleasantly now. The sheriff knew? Was taking payoffs to let these guys work from here? Jesus, Joe, this just gets worse by the damn minute. Joe lifted his hands to his face, pressing the heels of his hands against his eyes. This can't be. Whatever it is, it can't be this.

The sheriff said, "We have to find this guy,

see what he knows. And you guys are gonna have to move. Too many questions, now. I know of a couple of other places you can use, temporarily at least."

"We have a few houses, one a couple of hours from here. We'll head there as soon as we find this guy. We're gonna have to burn this place, though." Peavey stepped closer to the sheriff, and Joe leaned forward, struggling to catch the man's words.

"You want to keep your nice little bonus coming, you'll find us another place in the area soon."

"Yeah, I hear you. Now let's find this asshole."

Peavey turned toward the woods and the sheriff took the long flashlight from his car and shined it into the trees. Joe knew the failing light would make shapes in the semi-dark woods indistinct, helping to hide him, but he pressed himself as low to the ground as possible.

"I'll start in here, you go down about twenty yards and work your way back."

"Yeah, fine," Peavey said, followed by footsteps. It was obvious from his tone that he disliked taking orders.

Joe could see the light moving closer when he heard a voice from the police radio.

"Sheriff, there's been an accident on Broadcut Road. Looks like Mark and Allan Purliss flipped their truck, again."

Joe heard the man say, "Son of a bitch. Okay, I'm on my way. You have EMS in route?"

The small, tinny voice from the radio clipped to his shirt said, "*Already on their way, Sheriff.*"

"Peavey, I've gotta go. Find this jackass and take care of him! Let me know when it's handled."

From further down the row of trees, closer toward the house, Peavey replied, "Whatever."

The sheriff slid back into his car and disappeared from Joe's sight. The car backed out of the drive, the siren came on, and the car was gone.

As it always seemed to Joe, once night approached, it came quickly. Nighttime was always the worst. Being alone in the house, his thoughts running toward his ex-wife and daughter, with only the T.V. and a few beers to help slow them down. Now, he was stuck in the woods, and the shouting voices of the searching men reminded him he was far from home and even farther from alone.

He could see lights coming on through the trees, including a bright bare bulb shining from the front porch of the house now.

One of the men shouted, "Hey, do we have a flashlight?"

"Use the one on your phone, dumbass."

"Can't find my phone. Might have left it in the van."

Joe's mind spun as footsteps approached the van. He could see almost nothing but lights through the trees now.

"I can't find the damn thing! One of you call

it! I might have dropped it."

Joe could tell it was Peavey's voice that said, "Mike, you're an idiot. David, call Mike's phone!"

"Yeah, ok," David responded.

Joe tore the phone from his pocket, his only thought, No, oh shit no. Shut it off, shut it off, Joe. He remembered that his phone would always play a short musical cue when he shut it down. Pop the damn battery.

Joe wedged a fingernail into the seam on the bottom edge of the phone and pulled. The plastic crackled as it came loose, and he cringed at the noise, glancing up to see if lights were coming his way.

He dropped the thin plastic and tried to get his fingers under the battery, pop it loose.

His hands were washed with light when the screen lit up and the phone began to ring, as loud and obnoxious as the old rotary dial phone that used to hang on the wall in the kitchen of his youth.

Joe groaned a sound of utter fatalistic terror and muttered, "No, no damn it, no." He felt sick again, and he didn't think it was possible, but his heart began to slam even harder in his chest. He felt like weeping. This isn't supposed to happen, he wasn't supposed to be here.

When he heard one of the men shout "There, in the woods!" he dropped the phone, stood up and plunged further into the trees, in the direction of the road they had turned in from.

Joe seemed to bounce like a pinball from

tree to tree, tripping over vines and underbrush. He stumbled over a log, and his head connected with a tree trunk, sending him to the ground. Blood began to pour down his face, and over the ringing in his head he could hear as well as feel pounding footsteps coming toward him. The men with lights fared much better in the dense, dark woods.

Three tall shadows loomed over him, lights blinding him to their faces. A foot swung out and connected with the same spot that had hit the tree and all was darkness for Joe Pruitt.

Chapter 11

First, there was pain and only pain. Then, there was the recognition of darkness. Darkness and agony. The world beyond his eyelids no longer existed. Only the searing, pounding nightmare inside his skull. The darkness was the confidant to which he confessed his weakness and terror. Throbbing torment was its only response.

Sounds began to filter through; shouts, whimpering cries, exhortations of violence. It all came from somewhere that meant nothing to Joe Pruitt, a place that bordered on reality, and only offered suffering.

Joe groaned in pain.

A voice in the void said, "Hey Peavey, he's waking up."

Something pressed under Joe's chin, tilting his head up. His right eyelid popped open, pried by foreign fingers. Bright light from a bare bulb singed his retina and he flinched, pulling away.

"Guhh." Was all he could muster.

"He's gettin' there. Grab me a bottle of water from the cooler."

Frigid water smacked Joe in the face and he jerked again, trying to avoid the cold and the wet. The chair he was in began to topple backwards, and Joe tried to fling out his arms to catch himself. They wouldn't move.

His brain processed "Tied up," just before the chair went over and the back of his head bounced on the hard floor covered in cracked linoleum. Another burst of pain, spots in front of his now-open eyes, another "Guhhhh," followed this time by a "Fuuuuh."

"Chatty fucker, isn't he?" Joe already hated the sound of that voice, one that, even in his current state he recognized as that of the man called Peavey. "Get him up."

Shadowed men loomed again, and his chair was yanked up from the floor. His stomach dropped and for a single moment he felt weightless, as if he were spinning through space, moved by the hands of an angry, dark god. His legs were unbound, and he placed his feet on the floor to steady himself as they set the chair down.

As soon as his chair was upright, he was doused with more cold water. This time he didn't jerk, only sputtered. He tried to toss his head, fling the water from his face, but the sudden movement instantly made his vision swim and darken, the headache pressing like a shifting weight inside his head, bouncing side to side with incredible force.

Tears began to slip from his eyes, and deep inside he hated himself for letting the fear and hurt tear him open and expose his weakness to these men.

Standing in front of him Peavey said, "Hello Mr. Joe Pruitt, glad to have you finally awake and in the present. I'd like some answers from you, and I'm not gonna make idle threats to impress you, I don't have the time. Because of you, we have to move our entire operation tonight, and I'm not very happy about that."

Peavey stood next a kitchen table that looked to be from a 1970's sears catalog, on which sat a laptop computer and a rusty hammer. He reached out, picked up the hammer, and held it up in front of Joe's eyes. "I'm not gonna to make threats. Here's what's gonna to happen; you're simply gonna to tell me how you found us and who you're with. If you don't I'm gonna hit you in the face with this hammer. That's not a threat, Mr. Joe Pruitt, that's simply what I'll do."

Joe's vision began to clear, and the warped, fuzzy edges around everything sharpened. He looked from Peavey, to the hammer, and to the man standing just to the right of Peavey. It was the porch-pisser and he did have a lip piercing. A perfect little ring with a small diamond gem.

A quick glance around the room showed him that this was a temporary, but well used base. They must work this region often enough to need one. Several sleeping bags on cots, a cooler, a camp cooking stove with a propane bottle. There was random trash thrown about, proving it was a waypoint, probably no more than a few days at a time when they were in the area, nothing more.

Joe looked back at Peavey and took a second to study the man. He observed the tight, slightly pinched face with a mop of dark brown hair. His bottom lip was tugged to the side with thick, jagged scar tissue. His eyes seemed like they were a fraction too small, and they were just a little too close together. They were dark eyes, not in color, but in menace. Joe could see the torture this man would easily inflict if given the opportunity.

"I'm nobody," Joe croaked. "Just... just an average guy. I work for Fast Glass. I repair car windows. That's it."

Peavey bounced the hammer in his hand. "Just an average Joe, huh? Tell me, Average Joe, how did you end up on the back of my van?"

With his eyes going back and forth between the hammer and Peavey's face, Joe explained everything that had happened from the moment the van had screeched to a halt near the intersection to when they caught him in the woods.

He went silent and Peavey eyed him for a full minute without speaking. Then, "Well, that was easier than I thought. You really aren't some hard-ass cop or FBI, are you? I've met enough of 'em to know. You're just some dumb-shit hero wannabe. I'll be a son-of-a-bitch."

Peavey shuffled closer, lifted the hammer and pressed it under Joe's nose, pushing hard, forcing Joe's head farther and farther back until he was looking directly up at the ceiling. New tears dripped from the side of his face. Leaning over and looking down into Joe's eyes, Peavey said, "You've caused me a lot of trouble, Average Joe."

Peavey stepped back, raking the hammer over Joe's lip, tearing the skin. "Dave, Mike, get in here! Evan, stay right there."

Both Dave and Mike hurried into the room. Chiming in unison, "What's up, Boss?"

Using the hammer as a pointer he directed their attention to Joe. "You see this? Do you know why he's here? Because you two FUCKED UP!"

The men recoiled at Peavey's wild scream.

With two quick steps, Peavey crossed the room to Mike and Dave, and before either could react, he smacked each across the face with the flat side of the hammer.

One man's nose began to spout blood almost instantly, the other's face now sported a two-inch gash.

"When I send you out to pick up a specific little fat girl, you pick up that girl, and NOTHING ELSE! Jesus, you two shits could have cost us this whole damn job!"

The man with the bleeding nose, his shirt-front now soaked in red, whined, "Id wads Mike's frikkin' idea, Peavey, shid! He grapped her, sdarded feelin' 'er up and smagged her aroun' too when she bid 'im"

Joe glanced at the man with the gash and saw the hand he was pressing against the wound was wrapped in gauze. Had he not been in so much pain, and on the verge of screaming from terror, he might have grinned again at the girl's act of defiance.

"Screw you! You were driving. You didn't have to stop the van, asshole! You wanted to grab her as much as I did! Easy money, you said, easy friggin' money!"

"Shut the hell up, both of you!" Peavey ran his hand over his hair and glanced back at Joe. "We have to fix this, tonight." Still looking at Joe he said, "Get the girls gathered up and in the van. There's a holding house about three hours from here, Aikman has a few girls up there now. We can sit out at his place until the handoff."

Peavey turned to the one he had called Evan, the one Joe thought of as the porch-pisser. "I'll ride with these two jackasses and the girls in the van and make sure they don't screw anything else up, you take the truck out back." Peavey took a pen from his pocket and grabbed a scrap of paper from the trash on the floor. He scribbled something on it and handed it to Evan.

As Joe watched all of this, he was fully aware that Evan was being left behind to take care of him.

Handing the scrap to Evan, Peavey said, "The address for Aikman's place. Give us a twenty-minute head start, then kill this jackass and set the place on fire."

All the pain in his face and head seemed to wash away at the dawning realization that he really was about to be murdered by kidnappers that sold little girls. Squeezing his eyes shut for a moment, he said a silent prayer. Please, let me wake up now?

"You two, I want all four of those girls in the van and ready to leave in ten minutes. Clean your friggin' faces up and move."

Four? Four girls? Joe had only seen two. They had others here, and more at this Aikman's place. What does it even matter, I'm tied to a chair and about to die. Good God what was I thinking.

Joe realized that was the problem; he hadn't thought, he'd simply acted. If he had training, fighting skills, an arsenal of weapons or laser vision, he might have been able to help. The Joe Pruitt that was a good man, who wanted to do nothing more than help a young girl in trouble, was about to die because of the Joe Pruitt who leapt, without thinking, into the fire.

Were the two one in the same? Joe was certain he wouldn't have time to tease out an answer before a bullet smashed through his skull.

Chapter 12

Once Peavey had given his orders, he worked quietly as he closed and shoved his laptop into a leather satchel, along with a few papers which had been sitting next to it.

Evan left him tied to the chair in the filthy kitchen and went to help the other two men bundle the girls into the van for their trip to the Aikman holding house.

Just the thought of that, a *holding house* nauseated and enraged Joe. These people, building up a stockpile of "merchandise," which they kept locked away as if stocking the back room of a grocery store. They took orders for specific items and hunted them down with ease.

Evan, Mike and Dave packed the girls out one per man. Dave went first, and returned a minute later, retrieving the last one. Two of the girls wore blue jeans and t-shirts. The one he witnessed being snatched, the shorts. The last girl wore a skirt that hung loose, flapping under her as Dave walked past. Each of them seemed to slow their steps, as if gloating as they paraded by with their cargo.

Dave even cast a wink at Joe, who could do nothing but watch or look away.

Minutes later, Joe, alone and bound in the kitchen, heard voices from the porch. Peavey giving Evan a reminder on the time. Then, the jangle of keys.

Evan stomped back into the house and sat

down at the table dropping the keys beside him, he stared directly at Joe. Outside, the van roared to life, the sound of a dragon making off with fair maidens to be devoured. He could hear the tires crunching over dirt as it pulled forward, the headlights sweeping the house. Then it was dark outside once again, the red of the taillights faded and were gone.

Evan's face was lit by his phone as he stared at it, his finger occasionally flicking the screen. Maybe he was surfing social media, looking for fresh targets. Reading the news? Joe wondered if there was some group or message board where these bastards talked to each other, chatting and laughing about their recent grabs, or how much they made from the sale of a specific girl. He truly would not find it surprising. A kidnapper's version of Reddit.

Time seemed to drag, drawing out like putty, the wait to die a long and miserable one. Too much time to think and worry about pain. Wondering how it would feel to die, Joe twitched when Evan stood up. The man glanced at his phone once more and said, "Time's up asshole. Thanks for fuckin' up my night."

"Please man, please don't…" Joe looked into Evan's eyes as he began to plead for his life, and saw that this man was not only comfortable with killing, it was something he took some pleasure in. Life meant little to him.

Evan drew a pistol from behind his back.

Inside Joe's gut, in the middle of the fear induced nausea, a tiny but hot flame seemed to form out of nowhere. It was a flicker of rage beyond anything he had ever felt. The flame grew and became white-hot inside, burning away the terror he felt, distilling every emotion down to a crystal-clear moonshine of fury.

Evan stepped closer, raising the pistol, holding the barrel inches from Joe's forehead, as if needing to be as close as possible to the carnage he was about to create.

Right then Joe decided that if he was going to die, there was no way in hell he was going to go out with words of cowardice on his lips. He would not allow the universe to remember him as one who begged for his life, even in the face of certain death.

Joe decided to fight.

A faint grin began to spread across Evan's face as his finger tightened on the trigger.

Joe snapped out with his right foot, catching Evan in the left knee, at the same time shoving backward, tilting the chair, going over.

Evan's knee cracked and his smiled vanished. The sound of the breaking joint was lost under the roar of the pistol as he jerked the trigger.

Joe felt the heat and pressure of the bullet as it sung only centimeters passed his ear. He also felt one of the rear legs of the wooden chair crack and give way when he went over. He rolled over and got his legs under him, standing awkwardly.

Evan crumpled, and shouting his own rage, fired wildly from the floor. He took no time to aim, just snapped the trigger over and over. Bullet after bullet roared past Joe. He felt two tugs at his jacket, then a sudden searing streak like the edge of a hot iron being drawn quickly across his right love-handle.

"Damn it!" He shouted and fell again, going down to his knees this time.

Silence filled the air, then Evan roared in pain. The gun clicked empty.

Joe stood, turned, saw Evan fumbling with another magazine for the pistol.

"No!" Joe swung his entire body toward the man on the floor, the chair acting like a weight on a string, pulling him around.

Evan looked up just as the edge of the seat connected with his face. Bone cracked again, this time the bridge of his nose.

Joe was unable to halt his forward motion and he went tumbling over Evan, who had dropped the pistol and was now grabbing his bleeding face.

The second rear chair leg snapped in half as Joe tumbled. He stood, steadied his legs and charged at Evan, who was still on the floor. Joe was delighted to see that his last attack had not only broken the man's nose but had opened a wide gash across it and under his right eye.

Joe took two wobbling steps toward the injured Evan, turned his back to him, and loosed a wild, wordless scream as he flopped backward, leaning all his weight into the shattered back legs of the broken chair.

"GARRAAHHH!"

A gout of blood erupted from Evan's mouth with a grunted burst of air as Joe's full weight drove the broken remnants of two chair legs into his body. One into his chest, and the other into his gut.

Blood bubbled from Evan's mouth and pushed up around the wounds in his chest and stomach as the last of his life leaked way in a gurgling whisper.

Joe's heart felt like a raging gorilla trying to break free of the cage that were his ribs. He sat there for several minutes on the broken chair, on a man's broken chest, allowing his heart to slow, taking deep breaths and ignoring the tears leaking from the corners of his eyes.

When he believed his shaky legs would hold him, Joe stood. Forced into a lean by the chair, Joe stared at Evan's bloody face.

He had just taken the life of another human being. The man on the floor had, only moments before, been living and breathing, his heart beating and thoughts moving through his brain, plans, ideas and evil thoughts, most likely, but thoughts just the same. Joe had ended that. His gorge began to rise, his guts rolling at the sight of the broken, bloody, dead man. He fought it, resisted the urge to spew vomit over the body, and after several slow breaths, was able to get it under control.

He was conflicted, but knowing that the dead man had been evil of a special kind blunted the force of the emotional trauma that went with murder. Standing there over the body, Joe decided that what he had done *wasn't* murder. It was self-defense. It was retribution. It was vengeance.

Joe Pruitt began working his hands free of the rope that bound his arms to the chair.

Chapter 13

After several minutes of frantic jerking and twisting, Joe was able to get his hands free and shed the ropes binding him to the chair.

As soon as he was loose, he snatched the keys from the table and headed for the door. He ran the scenario through his mind, get to the truck, drive to the nearest town, find a policeman, get the girls the help they need.

Joe paused at the front door. He turned back toward the room he had just left. The body of Evan the porch-pisser lay there, a widening pool of blood spreading around his lifeless body.

The sheriff. The sheriff had been taking payments to let these people work out of the area. That money was blood money, made from the bodies of young girls sold and used. As terrible as the thought was, Joe wondered what happened to the girls after the buyers were finished with them. Were they traded off? Sent somewhere else, to live a dark and hateful life of sexual servitude until they died from a drug overdose or were beaten to death? Did they just cut their throats and dump them in a hole?

That image filled his mind, a pit, deep and black, filling with the bodies of girls used and tossed away. In that terrible glance from his mind's eye, he could see his own Cady Lynn being snatched from the street as she walked home from school or played on the playground. He could see faceless men standing around her, casting their bids. He imagined their hands on his daughter, stealing her innocence, her soul, then her life, her body being added to the pile, only to be buried by others soon after, gone, forgotten. Just one rotting corpse in an endless cycle of evil and abuse.

"No. No! NO!"" He screamed into the empty house. He stormed over to the dead body, his raw, violent screaming filling the space around him. Joe kicked Evan's body, blood spurting up from the man's mouth again, splashing from the hole in his chest, welling from the wound in his gut. For a minute that lasted a year, Joe lost himself to rage and hatred, and to self-loathing for his own perceived weakness, kicking and kicking until he heard bones crack.

Hands balled into tight fists as his sides, knees slightly bent, tilting forward at the waist, Joe's entire body seemed to clench into a compacted mass of rage. Thick tendons and veins stood out from his neck, his face turning crimson, Joe Pruitt screamed. "NOOOOOOO!"

One last kick, aimed squarely at Evan's face, another splatter and crack, and Joe was done. The bottom quarter of his pant-legs were soaked in blood, Evan's blood. I killed this man, he thought. Good.

Glancing at the table, Joe saw Evan's phone and the scrap of paper Peavey had handed him. Aikman's place. The holding house. Waiting until the hand-off.

Joe stepped over the body and grabbed the

phone and paper off the table. He felt a sudden, sharp pain in his side as he reached for the items. He tugged up his shirt and looked at the black and bleeding crease on his right side. He had been grazed by a bullet. The wound didn't appear to be severe. He dropped his shirt and left it. "Nothing I can do about it now," he muttered.

The bullet wound reminded him of the gun, and cast about for it on the floor, found it a foot away from Evan's hand. Picking up the gun, the weight felt almost foreign. Joe had been to the range with friends, even owned a shotgun and an old revolver that had belonged to his dad. He enjoyed shooting but had never been as into guns as some of his friends. While familiar with this type of semi-automatic pistol, he wasn't entirely comfortable with it, having only shot one a few times.

He dropped the magazine, found it empty. There was one laying in a pool of blood next to the body. Pinching it between his fingers he lifted it free of the muck and wiped it on Evan's shirt-sleeve. He slipped it into the grip until it clicked, slapping the butt of the gun once to ensure it was fully seated.

The slide was locked back, and it took him several seconds before he remembered to hit the slide release. The gun jumped in his hand as the slide slammed another bullet into the chamber. He remembered to flip the safety up. He didn't want to accidentally shoot himself in the process of putting it into or taking it out of his pocket.

Joe wasn't about to shove the pistol down

the front of his pants like he had so often seen in movies. It was too easy to imagine the gun going off and blowing his man-parts away.

He glanced at the address and shoved the scrap of paper into a jacket pocket. He held up the phone and press a button on the side. The screen lit up without a password lock. The image on the phone was a grinning clown with a rotting face. Zombie clown. He swiped it away, revealing the home screen.

Joe nearly dropped the phone into the blood at his feet when it began to ring in his hand. A number with the capital letter "P" was the only caller identification. P for Peavey?

Joe let it ring out, thought for a moment, then opened the text-messaging app on the phone. A quick look at previous texts showed that Evan had a blunt style to his messages. He was someone who disliked texts.

What the hell, Joe thought. There were several older messages to "P", Joe opened the thread and, with shaky fingers, tapped in, *Asshole tried to fight. Phones messed up. Call won't go thru. Texts work.* He hit send and waited.

A chime, followed by the response, *Whatever. Are you driving yet?*

Lighting it now. Leaving one min.

Good. Keep an eye out for tails. See you at A's.

Joe responded with, "*K*".

He shoved the phone into his pocket, stepped over Evan's corpse one last time and went through the door into the night.

The truck was a newer model, with all the bells and whistles that went with a high-end pickup. Joe slid into the seat, slipped the key into the ignition and started it. Built into the dash was a touch-screen. Joe tapped at it until he got a GPS application. He punched in the address from the scrap of paper and waited while it found his route. Seconds later the screen showed him all the information he needed. The entire drive was two hours and forty-eight minutes.

Joe would have plenty of time to think. With knowing about the Sheriff, Joe wasn't sure who he could trust. Would they have someone on their payroll everywhere they had a holding house? Local police, county Sheriff, FBI? Joe wasn't sure he could trust any authority.

The only two things Joe felt he had left were forward motion and hope that he would come up with something. For now, Joe Pruitt would drive. And pray.

Chapter 14

A short while later, Joe turned from the gravel road onto a rough blacktop road, another mile after that he made another turn, which led him to a main highway. The truck rolled along, the steady thrum of tires on asphalt soothing. Joe searched the dashboard, familiarizing himself with the workings of the expensive vehicle. He saw a switch with a symbol that looked like a seat with wavy lines moving through it. Heated seats. He flicked the switch and within a minute smooth warmth radiated across his lower back.

He allowed himself to relax into the comfortable seat, but as his body shed the adrenaline he had been running on for the past few hours, Joe began to feel every point of pain.

His face hurt, the skin of his upper lip was tight, and it stung when he moved his mouth. Pain in his left hand, where it had been jabbed by a thorn or stick when he had first dived into the woods. There was a large knot on his forehead where it had connected with the tree in his attempt to flee in the dark woods. His lower back ached miserably, but the heated seat was easing that pain considerably.

Along with the aches and pains, Joe began to feel the hunger gnawing at his gut, and the dry cottony feeling of his mouth. The tastes of blood, sour vomit and road dirt mingled together, to create a pasty coating over his tongue and teeth. The slimy feel was unpleasant, and for a moment he wondered if this was what fear tasted like.

The armrest next to him was also a caddy. He popped the top and looked inside. Some folding money and loose change, a pocket knife that snapped open when he pressed the nub protruding from the back, a few fast food napkins, and two tampons. Joe's brow creased.

Tampons?

Yet another mystery, and one not worth considering at the moment.

He had just under three hours before he arrived at the Aikman house and still no plan on how to get help to those girls.

Right then, Joe wanted nothing more than something to drink, a handful of painkillers, a sandwich and a toothbrush.

He picked up the folding money and counted thirty-eight dollars. The fuel gauge showed the truck was almost topped off. Maybe he could afford a short detour.

Joe jammed the money into a pants pocket, along with the knife. Never know when a blade might come in handy.

Joe had driven thirty-five miles before he spotted a sign for an all-night fuel stop. He took a right off the highway and drove another mile before he spotted a small but brightly lit store with 6 fuel pumps and few vehicles. It wasn't a big-name truck-stop, probably a mom-and-pop place, just far enough off the beaten bath to keep itself open without being overly busy, even at nine in the evening.

Joe pulled the big pickup into a lined

parking spot near the front doors, shut it down and hopped out. He considered his blood-soaked pant legs and shook his head. He hoped the dark blue of his work pants would hide the blood, at least a little. There was really nothing he could do about it at this point.

Inside, the store was brightly lit. The two clerks, a female, brunette, maybe mid-twenties and a man who looked to be a few years older than Joe, maybe early forties, both nodded at him when he came through the door that announced him with a cheery chime.

Smells of coffee and hot-dogs on heated rollers hit him as soon as he stepped through the door. The hum of the cooler section, ice dropping in the fountain-soda machine, the white-tiled floor, cracked in places. With all the traveling he did for Fast Glass, shops like these, big and small, had become familiar, and it was now a source of comfort.

The woman smiled, "Evening. If I can help you find something, just let me know."

"Uh, thanks." Can you help me find The Punisher, or Superman, lady? Joe kept the thought to himself and moved through the cozy store. In a narrow aisle, he picked a cheap travel toothbrush, the kind that fit into its own handle, and a small travel-size of toothpaste. Then he made for the cooler section, where he grabbed two large bottles of water. He passed a hot-case on the way to the front and spied a couple of pre-packaged burgers. He added those to his purchases. Next to the hot-case were several pots of coffee, and he was happy to see that they still used the glass pots, not those pump carafes. Joe wanted his coffee hot. He had to set his purchases on the front counter before getting coffee, and he really wanted coffee.

There were only two other shoppers in in the convenience store, a younger couple. The girl had several bags of chips, and the boy carried a case of cheap beer. With their soft, and slightly familial features, Joe thought they could be brother and sister. As he passed them, the young man squeezed the girls' butt, and she giggled, slapping his hand. Then again, maybe they weren't related, at least, Joe hoped not.

With his other items on the counter, Joe went back and selected the largest disposable cup they had, filling it with the darkest coffee available. He would normally drink it black, but he added six packets of sugar, hoping that the caffeine and a sugar buzz would keep him going for at least a few more hours.

As he was pressing the plastic lid onto the cup, Joe heard the male clerk say. "Need to see I.D. kids."

The young man responded, "Yeah, sure."

The door chimed again, and Joe glanced up.

Two people came through the door, both wearing ski masks.

Joe's first reaction was a whispered "Oh bullshit."

Joe ducked down below the coffee station, hoping he hadn't been seen. Are you freaking kidding me. This is *not* happening, he thought.

As the scene played out in the front of the store, Joe wondered, briefly, if this robbery would even be happening if he hadn't stopped here. Had his jumping on the back of that van started some insane butterfly-effect that now spiraled out around him, acts of violence that maybe wouldn't have happened now occurring simply because he had done something so out of the ordinary that it had thrown the balance of the world off by a degree.

I should be at home, watching T.V., sipping a beer. Falling asleep while reading a magazine. This kind of shit doesn't happen to normal guys like me.

The robbers were yelling about money, the girl was screaming, the young man was shouting "Keep your fuckin' hands off her!" The clerks were saying "We can't open the safe! We can give you what's in the registers, but we can't open the safe!"

Joe slipped his hand into the jacket pocket and fingered the pistol resting there. You're no hero, Joe Pruitt. Hide, let it go down, and get the hell out.

The sound of a shotgun cocking brought Joe completely into the moment. He placed his freshly poured coffee on the ground, slipped the pistol out and flicked the safety off with his thumb. His hands were already shaking. How in the hell was he supposed to take on two armed robbers?

Killing Evan had required no thought. It was a do or die moment. Joe wasn't sure he could pull the trigger on another man in this kind of situation. He knew he didn't want to, but as the night had already proven to him, what he wanted meant nothing to the universe.

Joe scanned around the store from his crouched position. He could see an exit sign and the top part of a door toward the back, above a shelf that stood in his way.

Just duck-walk my back there, ease the door open and slip out unnoticed. Open the door loudly, hide and wait for one of the robbers to come to the back to investigate, hold him at gun-point. Stand up and just start blasting away with the pistol, even though he only had eight bullets.

Joe ran each scenario through his mind several times, before vetoing each. He sucked in a deep breath and stood slowly, inching up just until he could peek over the coffee station and hot-case, hoping the robbers were looking toward the front of the store and their captives, not toward the back.

They were still yelling at everyone. The boy was scowling in rage at the man holding the shotgun inches from his face. Brave kid. Or stupid. The other robber was pointing a hand-gun at the clerks behind the counter. The criminals stood within arm's reach of each other.

Joe was ten feet from the counter, but he would have to come around the aisle and take at least three steps before he was close to the gunmen.

Joe ducked back down, glanced at the pots of steaming coffee and paused long enough to think, you have to help those girls. You aren't gonna survive long enough to help anyone.

With only the smallest kernel of a plan, Joe slipped the pistol back into his jacket pocket, stood and grabbed a pot of coffee in each hand.

Chapter 15

"Hey, if you're guys' coffee taste like it smells, then this stuff is bad or something."

Every eye turned to Joe as he came around the end of the aisle holding the two pots. He kept his eyes down, like he was looking at the coffee, but he could tell when the man with the shotgun swiveled, pointing the gun at him.

"Stop right there asshole!"

Joe kept moving. He only needed four steps to get close to both robbers. Each step was a silent prayer that neither of the men was truly itching to shoot someone that night.

"Hey, dickhead, he said stop!"

Still looking at the pots, Joe said, "You guys might want to make some fresh coffee."

As soon as he was close enough to reach, the shotgunner jabbed him in the gut with the barrel. Joe let it push him a half-step to the side. He now stood slightly in front of and between both robbers. "Hey, what the hell!" he said, feigning ignorance of the situation.

The shotgun was still pointed at his gut, but he could see that the other man had let the pistol drift, and it was now aiming at a glass surface under which numerous rows of scratch-off lottery tickets sat instead of at the female clerk.

If this is what being a hero is, it sucks. Joe swung both pots of steaming coffee up as hard as he could, and stepped forward at the same time, hoping to avoid a blast from the shotgun. The one with the pistol was angled away from him, and the pot caught him on the right side of his face, shattering, the coffee instantly soaking through the mask. His screaming began a half-second before the shotgunners did.

The shotgun fell to the floor with a clatter when the coffeepot exploded square on the man's nose, sending hot liquid and shards of glass into his eyes. He clasped his hands to his face and dropped them again almost instantly, his feet pumping up and down as if he had suddenly been struck by the need to flash dance.

Joe could only imagine the intensity of that pain.

The boy, who was still holding the beer, dove forward and used it like a battering ram, slamming the heavy case into the pistol-holder's face. He fell backward, crashing into a rack of cheap sunglasses. The pistol roared once, the bullet firing almost straight up into the ceiling.

Joe was about to reach in and grab for the pistol when the young man dropped on top of the pistol shooter and began pummeling him, his fists pumping up and down like angry pistons, driving over and over into the masked face. The robber had gone silent, most likely unconscious.

"Enough, Donnie! Stop!" The girl was pulling on Donnie's shoulder and the boy relented, his knuckles already raw and bleeding.

Crying, chattering, words of thanks from the male clerk. Joe saw the female clerk on the phone, heard her say, "Some guys just tried to rob us…"

She had called 911. 911 meant police, and Joe would have to answer questions, questions that could take hours. What if they were on the payroll of men who trafficked in young girls?

Without a word, Joe turned and headed for the door, forgetting about his purchases. A voice behind him said, "Hey, Mister, your stuff!"

Turning, Joe saw the male clerk shoving the items he'd sat on the counter into a couple of plastic sacks. He muttered, "I'm good."

"Seriously man, thank you. Just take it, please."

Instead of arguing, Joe stepped around the moaning robber that had been carrying the shotgun, took the bags from the clerk and paused, then he walked back to the coffee aisle and grabbed the cup he had left there. Might as well.

Heading for the door, he looked at the male clerk and nodded, "Thanks. I can't be here when the uh, cops… arrive. Sorry."

The clerk nodded and Joe once more headed for the door. He stopped next to the groaning robber, looked at the shotgun on the floor for several seconds, then bent over and scooped it up with the hand holding the bags of groceries.

Without another word, Joe Pruitt stepped through the door into the night and was gone. The cheerful chime from the door was a strange counterpoint to the violence that had just taken place.

Chapter 16

Back on the road, Joe popped open a bottle of water, rinsed his mouth and spit it out the window as he followed the guidance of the GPS system. Before tearing into the food or sipping his coffee, he took a moment to squeeze a pearl of toothpaste on the travel toothbrush and scrub hard at the nasty film coating his teeth and tongue.

With that done, and another mouthful of water to rinse, Joe took a test sip of the coffee. Finding it had cooled sufficiently, he took long, deep drink of the sweet, bitter brew, savoring the flavor and warmth. He was careful to sip from the side of his mouth. His lip still stung where Peavey's hammer had gouged it.

For the second time that night, Joe Pruitt had to allow himself several minutes to come down from the rush of adrenaline, although this time was far easier than the last. The sugary coffee seemed to help steady him.

He reached into one of the plastic sacks and fished out a burger wrapped in thick, white, waxy paper. He tore the wrapper away, and bit in. Joe winced at the pain in his lip, but it couldn't be helped, and two minutes later he was taking his first bite of the second burger.

It was a good thing no one was around to hear his grunts and groans of pleasure elicited by the food and the coffee. Simple things he had almost daily, unremarkable on their own, took on a new meaning when only hours or minutes earlier he had been on the brink of a violent death.

As Joe chewed his way through his sandwich and drove the truck through the night, following the beams of light spearing out in front, he contemplated the situation waiting for him at the Aikman house.

He knew of three men, Peavey, Mike and Dave. Possibly this Aikman person. It stood to reason that if Peavey was the leader of his little group, Aikman may have his own band of henchman, though how many Joe couldn't guess. If he ran his bunch the same as Peavey, then he might have three. Which would leave him up against seven men. All of whom were persons without a moral code. If they could kidnap young girls and sell them for profit, then killing a single man who risked their business would be nothing more than a minor inconvenience.

Joe tossed a quick glance at the phone now resting in the console beside him. What options do I have? he wondered. Local and county police were completely out of the question.

Again, he considered the FBI, but if it was a local branch there was no guarantee that they weren't also on the payroll of these men. Joe had no clue how far their reach went, nor how much money they had spread around to protect their interests.

He was sure that money was one thing they had in abundance. Trading in people was profitable. Selling young people was probably even more lucrative, he thought.

Chapter 17

The night rushed by on both sides of the truck, and Joe settled into the drive. Other vehicles would occasionally zip past him, or infrequent headlights from the two far lanes would appear, pass and be gone in moments. As the night grew on, traffic thinned, and the dark highway became darker and lonelier.

The thought that he was on his own, barreling down a highway toward murderers and kidnappers, without any back-up, no one to come to *his* rescue should he need it, (and he was certain he would) kept bouncing around in his head. Repeatedly, he questioned himself, his actions and his motives. There was nothing to gain from rushing headlong into a situation he had little hope in escaping. The girls needed help, but he couldn't help them. He was surely to die.

Joe's foot relaxed on the pedal and the needle on the speedometer began to drop. He could turn around, right now. Find someplace to ditch the truck, hitch a ride back to his work vehicle, and go home. He could make an anonymous phone call, and forget he ever saw anything at all.

It would be the easiest way. Leave it all behind and go back to his simple life.

Would it ever be that easy, though? Could he ever forget? Everything seemed to be "If."

If he called the authorities, would they be on

the take?

If they weren't, would they get there before the girls were moved, or sold off?

If they didn't, could he ever live with himself?

Another thought began to form, one that was equally as terrifying.

They knew Joe's name. They could find him. If they could find him, they could find Cady Lynn. If they found his daughter, they could use her to get to him, to punish him.

Joe's foot dropped back to the gas pedal and the needle began to climb once more.

Whether he wanted to be or not, Joe was in it to the end, whatever that end might be.

Before he could talk himself out of it, Joe picked up the phone and dialed one of the few numbers he had committed to memory years ago.

Several rings later he pulled the phone away from his ear and was about to press the end button when he heard a tiny voice say, "Uh, hello?"

Pressing the phone to his face again, he said, "Hey, Paul?"

"Yeah, this is Paul. Who is this and why the hell are you callin' me so late?" The voice on the other end sounded thick, as if the speaker had been woken up from a deep sleep.

"Hey, Paul, buddy, it's Joe. I'm sorry to wake you up, man."

"Joe?" Paul's voice seemed to instantly come alive. "Jesus, Joe! What the hell's going on? I've tried calling you like ten times.

Cassidy's pissed because you abandoned your truck. He says you haven't been answering his calls either. He even notified the police. I don't recognize the number you're calling from, either. Almost didn't answer."

"I'm glad you did. Listen, man, I really can't explain everything right now. Tell Cassidy I'm sorry. On second thought, don't tell Cassidy anything."

"Joe, buddy, what the *hell* is going on?"

"I've kinda fallen into a bad deal. Well, jumped into is more like it. I really can't tell you much, brother, for your own safety."

"Bullshit. I've had your back since we were kids and you and your family were unloading your moving van on our street. Whatever it is, I can help."

Joe sighed, contemplating for a few silent seconds telling Paul everything, enlisting his help. But Paul had two kids of his own, a boy and a girl that called him Uncle Joe, and a marriage that seemed to be doing better than most anyone else's Joe knew.

"I can't, Paulie. I wish I could tell you, but I can't. I'll say this, I tried to be a good Samaritan, help some people who really need it, still am actually, but it might be…" Joe was unsure how to finish the sentence. "There *is* something I need you to do for me, though."

"Yeah, buddy, anything."

Joe glanced at the dashboard. It was just after 10 o'clock. "If you haven't heard from me in twelve hours, I need you to do a few things for me."

"If I haven't heard from you? Damn it, Joe, talk to me!"

Joe felt heartsick at causing his closest friend so much anxiety. He wouldn't if he believed there were any other choice. Quickly, unequivocally, he told Paul everything he wanted to say, without letting his friend interrupt. "First, you call the TV stations, give them these names, and locations." Joe quickly rattled them off. "Second, whatever you do, do *not* call any law enforcement branch until *after* you've called the tv stations. Tell them a human trafficking ring has been operating in the area. To both the TV people and the cops, tell them about a specific girl." Joe described the girl he saw grabbed and thrown into the van. "That should help prove the story. You need to do all of this anonymously. Don't give your name, use a throw-away phone that has no connection to you, whatever you have to do to keep it from being connected to your name."

Joe took a deep breath, and Paul broke in. "Good God, buddy, what the hell have you gotten into?"

"I hope I can tell you about it, soon, man. I really do. The third thing I want you to do is…" Joe paused, his voice breaking around the tight, painful lump that had formed in his throat.

"Joe?"

"I need you to call Cady Lynn… tell her I love her. Tell her I'm sorry things turned out the way they did, with everything. I tried to be a good dad, Paul."

Everything swam in front of Joe, the world distorting as if seeing it through a storm-lashed window. His voice broke again, and hot tears dropped from his eyes. In the back of his mind he was thinking that men weren't supposed to cry, and how he had shed several tears over the course of this bleak and violent night.

"Make sure she knows I loved her very much, Paulie. Please. And tell Anne I'm sorry, too. I screwed up too many times, didn't pay attention, spent more time working, when I should have been at home. I thought that was how you took care of them. Just, please, tell them. Make sure Cady Lynn knows, ok?"

Joe heard the crack in Paul's voice. "Joe, dammit, you're talking like you're already dead."

"I might be, Paulie. I don't know what I'm doing, and fuck if I'm not scared to death. I don't want this. I don't want anything to do with it, but I don't really have a choice anymore."

"Bullshit, Pruitt! You have a choice, call the cops, let someone else deal with it!"

Joe heard a sleepy female voice in the background ask, *"Paul, what's wrong with Joe? What's going on?"*

"One more thing, Paul. Do *not* call this number back. I'm gonna delete this call from the history. If something happens, I don't want them connecting it back to you. I mean it. They'll hunt you down and kill you if they know."

"Joe, don't man, please, let…"

"Hey, Paul, I…"

A long silence, held for several heartbeats, then Paul said, "I know, man, me too."

"Goodbye, Paulie." Joe pulled the phone way from his face, its surface wet with tears, and tapped the end button. He placed the device back in the console and leaned back in the seat.

The sobs came hard and fast, like three quick punches to the chest. Then he wiped his face dry, sucked in several deep breaths, and glared out the windshield, eyes on the highway lit by high beams.

He picked up the phone again and took a minute to tap his way through the screens, erasing the history of his call. With that done, he focused on the road. He now only had about forty minutes before he reached the Aikman place.

His detour for coffee and food had let the crew in front of him get even farther ahead, and he was sure they would be getting to the holding house shortly, if they weren't there already.

Though Joe was now concerned with protecting his daughter, he hadn't forgotten about the girls in the van.

To the windshield and the night beyond he whispered a prayer. "Lord, help me."

Chapter 18

Joe pushed on into the darkness, headlights and a GPS his guide to what, he believed, might be his own death. The moon was nearly full, the sky clear and filled with stars. He wished he were up there among them, above all the pain and fear he felt.

As he drove, Joe took stock of his very small arsenal. A shotgun with four shells, the pistol with eight rounds he had taken from Evan, and a single spring-loaded pocket knife.

More than enough to taken down an entire enemy fortress if he were the star of an action movie. Enough to take out a small group of bad guys if he were a trained soldier, proficient in combat.

But Joe Pruitt was untrained. Like any number of men, he had been in his fair share of fist-fights. He had even walked away from several still standing, while the other guy lay out cold on the ground, though he always wondered if that was as much due to the booze they had been consuming as how hard he hit. A shot or two of good whiskey would be damn nice right now, Joe thought.

With his meager weapons of war arrayed in the seat next to him, Joe glanced at the GPS. Less than fifteen miles to go. He would be making a turn soon, off the highway.

He jerked when the phone chimed into his silence. The screen lit with the notification of a message received.

Where the hell are you?

Joe let off the gas pedal a little, letting the heavy truck slow. Under any other circumstance, he would have ignored the message until he was stopped somewhere. But the current situation was about as far from normal as he could think of.

He punched in *Coffee and a piss. Almost there*, and hit send.

It was at least a full minute before the response came.

There's a gate. Pull up, flash your lights 3x, will let you through. Park near gate and wait. Make sure you weren't followed.

K

There was no further response, and Joe dropped the phone back in the console.

His heart began to thump harder as he made a turn onto a blacktop road off the highway. He followed this for several miles before making another turn onto a gravel lane. Two more turns followed, and he was once again in the middle of nowhere, trees and fields surrounding him on every side, rough gravel crunching beneath the wheels of the truck.

Despite the headlights of the truck and the brightness of the moon, the world seemed to darken to Joe, just a little at the edges, as he pulled up to a metal gate. He stopped inches from it and thumbed the light switch three times.

In the distance, down a gravel lane, he could see the upper floor of a farmhouse. He was unable to make out any details of the house, other than lights that were shining in most of the windows.

The gate was set into stone pillars erected on either side of the graveled drive. A low wall of stone extended about twenty feet on either side of the pillars, and past that was just woods. He could see down the lane that the drive cut through thick trees for several yards before widening out into what looked like a circle drive, although he was unable to see all of it from his location.

With the warm night, Joe had the window down and heard the buzzing of the electronic lock seconds before the gate popped open and swung inward. He guided the truck through, and once he was far enough past, he pulled the truck to the left side of the drive, shut off his lights, and killed the engine.

The sudden silence of the night around him, and the darkness of the cab of the pickup truck left an uneasy pit in Joe's stomach. He was play-acting as a killer and kidnapper to gain access to this place, when, in reality, he had no clue what he was doing.

Sitting there in the dark, the moon and stars shining above the treetops of the surrounding woods, the isolation pressed in on Joe. He grabbed the shotgun, pistol, and pocket knife and flung open the door of the truck, needing to be outside, unconfined. With the overhead light on, he took a moment to slip the knife into a pants pocket, hooking the clip on the pocket seam, and he slipped the pistol into his jacket pocket once again.

Clutching the short-barreled shotgun, he reached back inside for one of his bottles of water. Now, standing there with the door open and the light on, he felt exposed and vulnerable.

He slammed the door, took his water and the shotgun and went to the back of the truck. Leaning against it, watching back the way he had come like the text message had said. Joe could only hope that someone had followed him.

After several long minutes of listening to the sounds of the woods around him, Joe turned to look back toward the house.

Down that lane, beyond those lighted windows, inside the walls of a building someone probably had called home once, long ago, waited several men who would be more than happy to end his life.

There were also young girls, more than four, though Joe had no way of knowing how many, being kept hostage, held for the highest bidder. One of the girls had even been ordered, like someone had chosen a style from a catalog. Had the man called someone and described his preferences? Was it done by internet, with a checklist or photos? All of this went through his mind as he stood there in the night, watching the house.

Now Joe Pruitt had to decide how he was going to proceed with his assault on the house and subsequent rescue of the captive girls. Even the notion of it seemed absurd to him.

Chapter 19

The men inside the house assumed he was Evan, and expected him to wait, to follow instructions. Eventually Peavey would summon him, or he would send another man down to replace him. Joe could wait for that man, and hope to take him out silently, or he could work his way toward the house and try to get a glimpse inside.

Knowing how many girls there were and where they were being kept would allow him to formulate a more detailed plan.

He could follow the lane on the right side, where the tree line wrapped around to the back of the house. It was still yards away from the building, but it would be preferable to crossing what amounted to a no-man's-land of what he imagined was a wider yard leading to the front door.

If he approached before being summoned and was spotted, Joe was sure the men guarding the house would become instantly suspicious.

One thing he knew for sure; he couldn't just stand there and wait. Time worked against him. He would be found out eventually. When he was found out, those waiting would be out for him in full force. And, they may try to move the girls again.

Joe wasn't certain of much at that moment, but one thing he was sure of; if Peavey and his group moved the girls this time, it would be the last time he would be able to locate them. Joe would either be dead or trapped.

Joe's feet scuffed gravel as he moved to lean against the truck, watching the house. One more minute, them I'm going in, he told himself.

Nearly five minutes passed, each bringing a new assertion that he would go soon.

As the sixth minute grew longer, Joe stood, collected himself and willed his heart to slow its erratic thumping. Toward the house or away from it, just move. Joe took a step out onto the graveled lane, in the direction of the house.

With a slightly wider view of the drive and the house, Joe caught a glimpse of shadow moving within darkness. Then the shadow separated from the night, backlit by a window from the house. The shadow parted, becoming two.

There was no more waiting.

Chapter 20

Two men were coming.

Joe glanced left and right. Woods on both sides. Deep and dark, and no light to guide him. They would see it anyway.

Frantic, his thoughts turned once more to simply running. By the time he was able to clear the low wall or the gate and run to the road, the men would be on him. Any action except inaction would bring nothing but suspicion.

Resigning himself to what came next, Joe Pruitt stepped backward, keeping his eyes on the shadow-walkers heading his direction. They were now on the gravel drive, and he could hear their footsteps kicking the loose rock as they came.

At the back of the truck, Joe sidled behind the tailgate, putting something between him and the approaching men. He bent his knees slightly, hunkering, hoping to minimize the target he gave.

When they were within two yards, one of the men spoke. He recognized Mike's voice.

"Hey Evan! Peavey wants you up to the house, man! Dave's gonna stay down here and watch the gate."

They kept walking as Mike talked. Joe's heart began to jump. His hands grew slick where they gripped the shotgun so tight that his knuckles were beginning to ache.

"Evan, you hear me, Peavey wants you!"

Keeping his voice low, attempting to mimic Evan's, he said, "Yeah," and nothing else.

Dave's voice, still distorted from the damage of the hammer-blow earlier in the night. "You god anymore covee?"

Coffee? "Uh, nope," he said.

They were now within twelve feet, the truck still between them and Joe. They were close enough for Joe to see by the moonlight that each was carrying a handgun.

Both men raised the pistols in Joe's direction. Mike said, "Evan hated coffee, dumbass."

The text he had sent earlier! They had known from that moment that Evan wasn't coming. Peavey had been waiting for him, letting Joe entrap himself.

With two pistols pointed directly at him, and the men still approaching, Joe was now down to the one element he hadn't been able to fathom earlier, at the gas station. Could he pull the trigger on another human being?

His hands shook. He was afraid he was going to drop the shotgun, but he was even more afraid that he was about to get a bullet in the head.

Joe's mind raced, disjointed thoughts ricocheting inside his head, all of them propelled by fear or anger. He had waited too long; the decision had been made for him. It was fight or die. Running was no longer an option.

"Peabey wunds you back ad da house," Dave said. That hammer had really messed him up.

Six feet away now.

From Mike, "Don't think we won't shoot you, asshole. Put your hands up and come out from behind the truck."

Five feet.

Joe had no idea what kind of loads the shotgun held. For all he knew, they could be nothing more than rock-salt.

He knew that if he were to go into that house with them, he would never leave it.

Joe ducked his head, scrunching his body lower behind the tailgate of the truck at the same time he brought up the shotgun. The two men approaching anticipated this, maybe they were even hoping Joe would make a move. Both handguns roared.

A bullet pinged into the tailgate. Another passed by, harmlessly a foot away. Their aim was off in the dark.

His hands were shaking so much, Joe didn't think he could hit anything narrower than a house even if he happened to be standing in front of it. He pointed the shotgun in their general direction and jerked the trigger.

Over the thunderous roar of the big gun, Joe heard a scream and a shout. Instead of glancing over the top of the tailgate, he slid to the side and peeked around the corner of the truck, almost resting his face on the tail-light.

One of the men was bent over the other, who was now laying still on the gravel. In the moonlight, Joe could see a pool of darkness spreading out around the man's head.

Move, Joe! Take control of the situation! Right now! He jumped up, shotgun held out in front of him, high, near his shoulder, ready to fire. "Don't move! Don't even friggin' move!"

With an animalistic growl, the man stood and charged at Joe, wild in his anger.

Joe, expecting the man to surrender, was startled by the attack and instead of firing, he backpedaled, feet skidding on the loose rock of the drive. The gun roared again when he accidentally jerked the trigger, firing nearly straight up into the night.

Then the attacker hit him, hard, a full body tackle. He shouted, "You killed Davey you sunvabitch!" Both men hit the ground.

Joe's shotgun flew from his hands, leaving him without an easily accessible weapon. The other man, Mike, his speech unaffected, brandished the pistol. Instead of shooting him with it, he whipped Joe across the face, driving the back of his head into the gravel.

Joe felt his skin split and pain like flame seared across the bridge of his nose. Sharp, small rocks dug into the back of his head. Stars leaped and spun in front of his eyes.

Peavey wanted to talk to him. Mike wanted to keep him alive. Joe knew there was no way in hell he was going into that house unless it was on his own terms.

With a guttural grunt, Joe shoved his hips up, bucking the heavy man on top of him. He balled his hands into tight fists, shouted "GAH!"

into Mike's face as the man leaned forward for another swipe with the pistol, and clapped both fists on Mike's ears as hard as he could.

The kidnapper nearly dove off him, howling with the pain, clasping at his own head, his pistol dropped and forgotten.

Joe rolled over, gravel digging into his knees and palms. His vision was blurry from the pain in his face and from the dry rock dust their scuffling had kicked up. He couldn't see his shotgun, or the pistol Mike had dropped.

Setting aside every thought but survival. Pushing away even the small voice in his mind that had previously made pulling the trigger difficult, Joe stood, blood dripping from the tip of his nose, took two shuffling steps and swung a kick at Mike's face.

The satisfying crack of bone didn't slow him. Mike rolled to the side, trying to get away from the onslaught. Joe took another step, kicked again, and connected solidly with the other man's right eye.

The angle and force of the kick must have been perfect, because the eye erupted in its socket. Mike howled again, the yell turning higher, becoming almost a screech. In any other situation, the sound and sight of the exploded eye might have made Joe nauseous. Now, it was just a moment of uncelebrated victory.

Joe huffed and sucked at the air, trying to draw a full breath through the haze of rock dust. He coughed and gagged, spitting a wad of pasty phlegm into the dirt at his feet.

"You and Peavey and whoever else's in that house can kiss my ass, buddy!"

From the ground, where he now hovered on weak hands and knees, Mike groaned and looked up at Joe. "You're dead. You're fuckin' dead, man."

Standing there, looking down on the man he'd done so much injury to, Joe was momentarily surprised to find a twinge of sympathy. Human suffering was never pleasant to look upon. Then he saw the gauze still wrapped around the man's thumb. He remembered what he had done to get the wound underneath it. The girl. All of them in that house. Waiting to be sold like livestock at market.

Something dark and unpleasant welled up inside Joe Pruitt. Another shuffle-step and he swung out with another kick.

Mike's head snapped backward and flopped forward, his face grinding into the rock as he fell flat. The man was out cold.

"Screw you," Joe muttered.

He glanced back toward the house, expecting to see the rest of the men waiting there charging down on him through the darkness, silhouetted like evil angels bursting forth from hell.

Nothing. No one came. They either thought he was dead, or they would wait for him to appear at the house with the other two bringing him in like some prize.

Once they did find out that Mike and Dave were both dead by his hand, Joe worried they would immediately try to move the girls, get them somewhere else. He couldn't let that happen.

No matter what, the kidnappers couldn't be allowed to leave. Even if he had to trap himself in with them.

Moving with a swiftness born of desperation and adrenaline, Joe ran to truck, slowing for a moment to witness the damage that he had done to Dave.

Most of the right side of his face was gone, the skin peeled away showing bone and muscle. A chunk of his skull had been ripped open and torn off, exposing brain tissue. The remaining good eye stared sightlessly up at the stars and moon. Silent witnesses to his crimes and his death.

With his stomach churning at the gory visage, Joe turned to the truck. He yanked open the passenger door and slid across the seat, lifting himself over the center console. He rammed the keyed into the ignition, turned it and fired up the truck.

Everything was a rush, hurry, move, waste no time. Someone would always be coming.

He pulled forward several feet, then shifted into reverse. The backup lights came on, showing the gate fifteen feet behind him.

Pressing the gas, the tires spun in the loose rock of the drive, then caught, and he rolled backward, gaining speed.

Suddenly, Mike was there, the red taillights and the backup lights turning his gore-covered face into a horror show. He had somehow found the fallen pistol and was now pointing it at the window of the truck now backing up directly at him.

The pistol cracked, a hole appeared in the rear window, a foot from Joe's head.

Joe jammed down the gas pedal and the truck lurched backward. There was no chance for Mike to leap out of the way.

The truck threw him back and he slammed into the gate seconds before the truck hammered into him again. The gate bent with the force of the truck, and Mike was crushed between the two.

Joe turned the truck off and jumped out. With the truck wedged against the dead man and the bent gate, it wouldn't be opening any time soon. He flicked open the pocket knife and ran around the vehicle, slicing off the valve stems of the wheels, glancing toward the house after cutting each one. Now the truck was sitting on four flat tires without an easy fix.

Standing there on the gravel drive, Joe glanced at Dave's dead body, then back to Mike, whose head now hung down far enough to touch the tailgate pinning him to the bent gate.

These men had both died at his hand. He had ended their lives.

Just this morning, even the thought of killing another human being would have been inconceivable. Now tonight, he had killed three. Him, Joe Pruitt. Glass repairer and divorced dad. Netflix binger and coffee drinker.

He thought he would be more upset by it.

Chapter 21

There was no time left to contemplate the horrors of the night. He grabbed the bottle of water from the truck, swished and rinsed his mouth, then took a long, deep swallow. The chill water made his dry throat ache. After drinking his fill, he upended the bottle over his face, emptying it. The water washed away the blood and caused his face to throb where the pistol had ripped open his skin.

I need an emergency room. What if I need stitches? He found a wad of napkins and pressed those to the bridge of his nose, staunching the blood. Though it hurt, Joe didn't think it was broken. In the movies, the tough guys just bled without worrying about it. Or, they gave themselves stitches with a makeshift needle and thread. He wasn't a tough guy, and this, sadly, wasn't a wild action flick on the big screen.

With the blood flow from his torn face slowed, he looked around for the fallen shotgun and the pistols the other men had been carrying. He found the long gun and racked the slide, ejecting the spent shell. Two rounds left in the shotgun. Dave's handgun lay near his bloody head, and Joe got to that just before the still growing pool of blood reached it. Mike's hand gun was gone. Most likely thrown far away when he was hit by the truck.

Every few seconds, he would toss a glance back at the house. He couldn't decide which made him more nervous; the fact that they were just waiting there at the house, that no one had come running to check out the gunfire, or the intense quiet of the night that seemed to backfill the void left by the gun shots.

The only option he felt he had now was to take his fight to those men. Someone had to do something, be that guy who acted instead of reacted. Joe wished silently that it didn't have to be him. Now, with just a few weapons, he would have to face off against men who were much better at killing than he could ever hope to be.

"Just hope someone up there is lookin' out for me tonight," he muttered, flicking his eyes to the night sky. He glanced at Mike's body and thought, maybe they already are.

With that, Joe moved toward the edge of the woods. Even though the moon was bright enough to light his way out in the open, the trees effectively screened the light out. He would have to stay at the very edge, no more than a few steps in, to be able to pick his way through the underbrush.

To Joe, the house looked to be about one-hundred fifty yards straight ahead. He could follow the tree-line, circle around to the back, and hope they would be watching the front of the house for his approach.

Instead of stepping in to the trees, he followed along them for a hundred yards, staying low in a crouching jog. He preferred not to waste time, since he had no idea how long Peavey and the others would wait before finally coming out to check on him, and picking his way through the undergrowth would slow him considerably.

When he was within fifty yards of the house, Joe pushed into woods, carefully moving the overgrown bushes out of his way, attempting to make as little noise as possible. Just a few feet in and he was still able to pick out his steps. He could only hope that he was no longer easily visible to anyone watching from the house.

It took him nearly fifteen minutes to make it to the tree-line directly opposite the house. There was still twenty yards from the trees to the building to move across.

Joe checked all around, and though it was possible to miss someone hiding like he was, a shadow within a shadow, he felt that he was alone and unwatched.

Moving with haste, he crouched and ran across the yard as fast as he was able, the shotgun clutched in two hands and held across his chest. It wasn't smooth, or pretty, but he reached the outer wall of the house unmolested.

He ducked beneath the dark window on the left, closest to the front corner of the house and waited until he got his breath under control before inching up to peek in through the glass.

A dim light shone through an open door across a wide room, and Joe ducked back down as someone walked past the light. His heart leapt into his throat and he waited a full minute before daring to look again.

The hallway beyond was empty. The light from the moon shining through the windows and the lit overhead fixture in the hall beyond let in enough light for Joe to easily view the room.

What he saw sent chills up his back and straight into his heart.

Chapter 22

Only a handful of people had ever crossed Anthony Peavey. Three were dead, their bodies disposed of in a way that they would never be found. Another was now a quadriplegic, every moment of his life requiring the assistance of a nurse, who, no matter how hard she or the doctors tried, could completely alleviate the pain he felt. Two others were in prison, one serving thirty-five years for double murder, the other a life sentence for the rape and dismemberment of four young men in New York City, though neither man had actually committed the crimes they had been convicted of.

Now there was Mr. Average Joe Pruitt, throwing a very big wrench into a normally smooth operation.

Peavey paced the kitchen of the farmhouse, his face a stone mask of rage. As the gunfire died off and the night beyond the house once again fell silent, he looked over to Aikman, who was sitting in front of Peavey's laptop at the round wood table. After the distant rumble of the truck started then cut off he asked, "Can you still hack the DMV or whatever it is you do?"

"Yeah, of course."

"Find out who this Joe Pruitt guy is. He said he wasn't with an agency, but I'm beginning to think that was bullshit."

Aikman nodded, "You have anything else? Where he's from, anything?"

Peavey just glared.

"It'll take a bit, but I'll see what I can find."

Peavey stalked out of the kitchen into the living room, where two men now sat, one on a worn sofa, the other in an overstuffed chair, a rifle across his lap.

"Get the hell up, both of you! Start watching the windows. We don't know jack shit about this guy, he may try to hit the house on his own. I want to see him before he gets close."

Both men glanced toward the kitchen, shifting in their seats, scowling.

Leaning forward slightly, Peavey said, "Don't look to him. I'm his fucking boss, which means I'm your boss."

The man in the overstuffed chair leaned forward and looked past Peavey toward the kitchen and called, "Aikman?"

From the kitchen came, "He's not lying. Do what he says!"

The man, whose face was half covered in tattooed scales, scowled at Peavey and stood. "Come on, Glenn."

The man on the couch joined him. They checked separate windows in the living room and left to continue throughout the house. Scales shot Peavey a look of spite as he left the room.

"And keep your hands of the merchandise!" Peavey shouted after them. Over his shoulder he said, "Where the hell did you find these guys, Aikman?"

From the kitchen, Aikman said, "Bolinger sent 'em down from Chicago as muscle. Was supposed to be teaching them the ropes so she could open a new supply line, but you had to bring this shit out here."

Peavey could hear the clack of keys as Aikman typed. He ran his hands over his brown hair, pulling it back and smoothing it flat. "Yeah, because this is what I wanted. Just find out who we're dealing with. Where'd your other two guys go, anyway?"

Aikman called out, "I'm not their babysitter, Peavey, shit. I think Nate's on the crapper. I told Porter to do a circuit of the house outside."

Peavey shook his head and stalked around the living room, looking through windows. After several more minutes of silence, he tried calling Mike, then Dave's cell phones. No answer. "Shit," he spat. How could the night have gone so far sideways?

"Peavey, come here."

Back in the kitchen, Peavey took up a position behind Aikman at the laptop, resting a palm on the back of the man's chair and leaning over him.

Aikman glanced over his shoulder at Peavey, then pointed at the screen. "Ok, so, thousands of Joe Pruitts, but I've narrowed it down to just the area here, say, about a one-hundred-mile radius or so. Anything else about the guy?"

Peavey took a moment to think, then said, "He's white, about five-foot eight or nine. Brown hair. He was wearing a dark blue pants and jacket. Like a uniform. I figured it was just his cover."

Tapping at the keyboard, Aikman asked, "Was there a logo on the uniform? A company name, anything?"

"If it's just a cover it won't matter."

"Yeah, but it's a place to start since we don't have anything else on the guy."

Peavey squinted, thinking, as if he could physically drag the memory out. "Two letters, F and G, with an arrow or line through them."

"What color were they?"

"Shit, Aikman, I don't know!"

Aikman took on a tone of placation. "Okay, okay, take it easy." He opened another browser window and tapped at the keys for a few seconds.

Peavey watched as Aikman scrolled down the screen. He jammed out a finger, pointing to an image. "That's it, right there!"

Aikman clicked the picture and it brought up a website for an auto-glass repair company. "Fast Glass. They repair and replace car windows. Pretty small operation. Looks like it's regional, to the mid-west. Hang on."

Several more clicks and he brought up the staffing page. Corporate, administration, field service.

Aikman clicked on field service. A list of fifteen people opened on a new page. Near the bottom of the list he saw the name *Pruitt, Joe* next to a photograph.

Peavey shouted, "That's him!"

Aikman ducked away, his eardrum close to

bursting.

Within minutes, Peavey knew who Joe Pruitt was. And who he wasn't.

"There's no way. This guy really is just some average asshole. That bullshit story he told about just happening to see Mike grab the girl and jumping on the back of the van wasn't bullshit." The incredulity in Peavey's voice was thick.

He wasn't sure how the information helped. Evan was dead, and he was certain that Mike and Dave were as well. How in the hell had this nobody killed three of his men?

Luck. It was the only explanation that made sense to Peavey, at all. The good Samaritan had gotten lucky.

A few bullets to the head had a way of changing a man's luck in a hurry.

Chapter 23

A room full of small beds. Girls tied to each, hands bound by rope or metal cuffs. One or two of the girls shifted in the beds, but most were still. To Joe, the idea that they were all just comfortably napping during the most terrifying moments of their lives didn't fit.

Exhaustion may force a few into sleep, especially if they had been taken over the past few days, but for all of them to be resting so easily, he didn't think it was possible.

Earlier, back in the van, one of the men, Dave, Joe now realized, had said to knock the girl out with chloroform and leave her alone. They were keeping them drugged.

It made a sick sort of sense. The girls would be far easier to move around, to handle, if they were drugged. Joe could only imagine the cacophony of crying and screams, as well. The kidnappers wouldn't want to listen to that for days on end as they moved the girls around the country to their final hand-off.

Gags wouldn't work either. If a girl vomited, she might choke. A dead girl made no money.

Joe was horrified by what he saw in that room, but even as he was processing it, he was appalled at how easily he considered their predicament and how the kidnappers were handling them.

This was the stuff of cop shows, police

procedural TV. He had spent many hours watching them, but maybe that was part of the problem. Too many hours in front of the television trying to block out the mundane nature of going through the motions of each day, a non-effort to not think about the hurt he had felt at Anne's betrayal, followed by the divorce.

Missing his daughter was even more difficult. Finding a numb place to simply not think had become normal, and the boob-tube was an easy click away on any given day.

Joe lost himself to painful thoughts, forgetting for the briefest moment his current predicament. Any soldier would tell you to keep your head on a swivel, always watch your surroundings. Cops know that people can appear out of nowhere with nothing but evil intent. The average person, without the proper training and skills, can lose themselves to the flood of emotions bearing down on them even in the direst of circumstances.

Joe Pruitt was lost in a moment of fear and sadness for his own life, and grief for the young girls bound inside that room.

The footsteps and a muttered "What the…" caught him completely off guard.

The man, just over six feet, with shoulders nearly as wide as Joe was tall, came around the back corner of the house, strolling casually.

Joe, hunkered down by the window on one knee, looked up just as the big man was raising a pistol in his left hand. Joe spun on his knee and rolled backward, an awkward somersault that saved his life.

The pistol fired, a thunderclap of violence, the bullet striking the corner of the house, missing him by a foot. Joe came out of his roll and bounced up, the shotgun still held across his chest. His head pounded from the roar of the pistol and the renewed pain of the sudden activity. He tried to bring the shotgun around, to trigger a round at the big guy, but he was too slow, the pistol roared again. Joe spun, the bullet tearing into the meat of his right shoulder.

He went down, and the shooter stalked toward him, re-centering his aim, coming for the final shot.

Joe knew the man wouldn't miss again. He rolled sideways in the damp grass, pulling the shotgun out from underneath his body. He didn't try to aim. He didn't even lift the heavy gun. Joe simply angled it in the man's direction and viciously jerked the trigger with the butt still on the ground.

The barrel was yanked to the right, and the roar of the shot seemed to split the very air itself. The big man grunted and slapped his right hand to his left side.

I hit him! Joe thought, and wasted no time regaining his feet. His own right shoulder was burning, and he led with it as he bolted away from the gunner, into the dark toward the trees.

Several more shots cracked, but none struck Joe. Would he even know if he were hit? If the shot was a fatal one, would it simply be running, then darkness and nothing?

He jigged back and forth, right and left, like a runner with the ball avoiding the big tackle. The woods were there and then he was crashing through, into the underbrush.

Over the noise of his thrashing through the trees, he heard a voice shout, "He's out here, just ran back into the woods!"

Another shout, this time from inside the house, muffled, unintelligible.

They were sending more men. How many did they have? Was it an army inside, just waiting to slaughter him when he got close? Was it a trap? Is that why they hadn't come running out when he was fighting Dave and Mike? Let the lamb come to the slaughter? Joe pushed blindly into the trees, going deeper, branches slapping at his face. One caught the wound in his shoulder and the pain was so sudden and surprisingly real that for a heartbeat he thought he was going to piss in his pants.

He still gripped the shotgun in his right hand, and his left flew up and pressed against the wound. He could feel blood flowing freely between his fingers, and down his arm, soaking into his shirt and jacket.

Behind him he could hear more shouts and the sound of others coming into the woods. It was impossible to tell how many there were. It could be just one or two, or, from the sound of men crashing through the trees, it could be an entire platoon of kidnappers, each of them hellbent on murder.

It was hard to hear over the sound of his

heartbeat in his ears, his own heavy breathing and his charge through the dark woods. He had to slow down. The trees helped in that regard.

He hit a tree with his left side, ricocheting off and slamming into another with his right shoulder. Pain, again, real and violent and full of its own kind of rage. The shotgun fell from his numb hand, dropping to the ground and gone, as if it had been swallowed by a hole that went all the way to the center of the earth. No time to find it.

Joe ran several more yards before coming to a massive oak twice as wide as he was. He ducked behind it, placing his back against it, toward the direction of his pursuers.

He believed, hoped, he had at least a minute or two before they got close. He squatted, pulling in great draughts of air, consciously willing his breathing and heart to slow.

The shotgun was gone. The pistol was useless in the dark, in Joe's hands, and with his heart beating as hard as it was, he didn't think he could hold it steady long enough to aim a decent shot. Not that he would have time to aim. He felt his pocket. The folding knife. He was certain wouldn't get close enough to use it.

On the ground at his feet were several pieces of long, dead tree limbs almost as thick as his wrist. The longest appeared to be about four feet. He could swing it like a bat and bludgeon the first man, but it would have to be a solid blow, putting the guy out of the fight.

Joe knew he couldn't evade the men for

long. Fighting two or more at the same time was certain death. Whatever he did, would have to kill or incapacitate instantly.

He listened to the kidnappers slamming their way through the trees, the lights from their phone's and flashlights playing across the limbs creating ghostly shadows that danced insanely among the trees like silent phantoms of death. The lights would disappear briefly in the rare spots of moonlight shining down through the tree tops.

The lights were getting closer. The men pursuing him made no effort to hide their position. They came smashing through the woods, and Joe found it disconcerting that they seemed so confident that there was no need for stealth.

Listening, watching the lights bob and weave through the trees, he waited. He hefted the length of dead wood in his hands and stood. One of the lights was closer than the other. He could hear footsteps, then heavy breathing.

Just on the other side of the tree, only feet away, a voice shouted, "Keep looking that way! He can't hide out here forever!"

Surprise. He still had that going for him.

Joe leapt out around the tree, brandishing the length of wood like a sword, gripping it with two hands, holding out in front. He wished he had a shield. A bulletproof one.

The man who had been searching for Joe was backlit by a shaft of moonlight piercing the trees directly behind him. Both men stared for an impossibly long second, the dark surrounding them like a shroud.

The man shouted "Porter, he's over here!" and lifted his phone higher, shining the light in Joe's face. Joe was half-blinded, but he could see the man's arm lift, the hand filled with a pistol. The gun popped, Joe felt wooden shrapnel pelt his face, and a tug at the length of wood in his hands. A quick glance showed him that the bullet had clipped the limb, ripping away almost a foot of the tip.

His weapon was now shorter, but the tip was ragged and pointed.

Joe shifted to the side one step. The gun popped again, the bullet missing him.

Two men, facing off, almost a firing line. Neither willing to give way. Except Joe was holding a stick. It was all happening too fast for Joe to think. He expected to have his skull shattered at any moment by a well-aimed bullet.

The kidnapper had taken several steps forward and was now less than eight feet away. Damn near close enough to touch, Joe thought. No time, he was about to fire another shot. Joe was certain the next would end up inside his head.

With a wordless scream of "NYAAHHHH!" Joe charged forward, no longer thinking, simply acting. Moving, because standing still meant he had given up, that he was ready to die, and Joe was not ready. The man cracked off another shot, missing Joe by inches, backed up two steps. Joe could feel the air shifting as the bullet whizzed by.

He raised the hunk of dead limb higher, pointing it directly at the man's face and charged forward.

The shooter was now standing in the full wash of a beam of moonlight. He tried to get off another shot, but he never pulled the trigger. His hand flew open and the gun dropped to the ground as the tip of the length of wood dropped a couple of inches and pierced his throat.

Joe was looking directly into the man's eyes as he pushed, harder and harder, until the wood stopped. Joe felt it hit the man's spine in the back of his neck. Blood sprayed around the ragged length of limb, splattering Joe's hands and face with hot, heavy droplets.

The look of utter shock and that brief moment of painful terror in the dying man's eyes was something Joe might never fully process. He was watching as the man died, while holding the weapon that killed him still embedded in the man's throat. Him, plain old Joe who had never been in more than a basic bar-fight before today.

Then Joe Pruitt opened his mouth and screamed that same wordless cry right into the dying man's face. Joe screamed his fear and hate, high and loud and as full of rage as he had ever been. Hatred for this kidnapper, for all of them.

Other than the rare drunken fantasy about beating Alan Fulsom to death with his bare hands for sleeping with his wife and stealing her away, Joe had never wanted to kill anyone.

Never had he thought seriously about murdering another human being.

Now, watching this man die, Joe felt a twinge of morbid satisfaction.

Then the man's head erupted in a fine red mist as a pistol shot cracked from off to Joe's left. The red mist seemed to hang in the moonlight for a moment as his mind processed what was happening.

He had forgotten about the man's partner, the one he'd called Porter. Porter was now trying to gun him down. His first shot had missed, catching his dead friend in the head.

Joe dropped the wooden shaft and let himself fall to the ground with the dead man, crumpling and rolling at the same time. That could have been my head. If Porter was a better shot, I'd be dead. Joe was sick of being shot at.

He wanted to wake up from this nightmare, right now. He wanted to go home. Take a shower, drink a beer. Maybe turn on a ball-game and lose himself in the game for a couple hours.

Instead, he rolled, jumped to his feet and dodged back around the massive oak. Bullets pelted the tree, and Joe took off at a loping run, dodging trees, ducking limbs, keeping the big life saving oak at his back between himself and the shooter.

"You're dead! You hear me, asshole! You're dead!"

You aren't the first person to tell me that tonight, Joe thought as he continued moving away from the voice, through the trees. How he wasn't dead was something he couldn't comprehend. He should be. Several times over already. Maybe his will to live was stronger than their desire to kill. Maybe it was nothing but luck. Divine intervention. Something beyond his own control.

But, he was alive, and he intended to stay that way.

Joe paused for a breath and listened. Porter was still coming, bashing his way through the trees. Joe couldn't run all night, and he had no idea how many men Peavey had in the house. He could keep sending them until they ran Joe to the ground.

Joe followed a random path for several more yards. He came up on a fallen oak, years dead. It was nearly as large as the tree he had been hiding behind only minutes ago. He slipped across instead of taking the time to go around.

On the other side, he slid to the ground and sat with his back against the rough wood. He could still hear Porter crashing through the dark woods like a wild animal. He had a few minutes before the man got close. He needed to breath, to think.

Joe turned and looked closely at the tree he was resting against. The light from the moon was enough to see that there was a pool of darkness on the underside. He slipped his hand under it and felt nothing but empty space for several feet. Leaves, dirt, small chunks of dry, crumbling wood.

Joe lay flat next to the tree and slid

sideways, pushing his feet under first, forcing them back until they stopped against something solid. He wiggled and shook his shoulders until his entire body was under the dead oak tree. Joe prayed that, either Porter wasn't close enough to hear, or that the other man's own noise covered that of his shifting into position under the deadfall.

It was a tight fit, and Joe quickly discovered that it was difficult to breath. The space was barely enough to fit his body. His back pressed firmly against the tree above him. Without enough room for his chest to expand properly, he could only draw shallow breaths, and every one of those felt like a chore.

Joe had never been claustrophobic that he knew of, but he couldn't help thinking that he had just forcefully shoved himself into a coffin that was three sizes too small. He squeezed his eyes tightly shut and concentrated on his breathing, focusing solely on drawing each successive breath.

After the first full minute of hiding, the mortifying thought that the tree was beginning to sink crept in to his mind. He was unable to push the thought away. Instead, his brain told him the tree was pressing even more firmly against his back as it sunk into the ground. His body would be lost forever, buried beneath a sunken tree. No one on earth would have a clue. He would be trapped, alone, in the dark, in the dirt, forever.

Joe's heart began to race even harder, fresh jets of adrenaline dumped into his blood, his breathing quickened, the tiny breaths coming hard and fast. He was about to scramble out from under the tree, unable to handle being trapped any longer, when he heard a voice.

"No, he's disappeared."

Joe stopped breathing, holding each breath as long as he could, listening. The tree vibrated against his back, like someone had jumped on it. Slowly, he released the air from his lungs and sipped another breath.

"Yeah, I'm sure Glenn's dead. Son of a bitch spiked him through the throat with a tree branch."

Porter. He was directly above him. Joe couldn't hear another voice, so Porter must be using a phone. Sitting, standing on the tree he now hid below?

Joe was convinced, in that moment, that the wild hammering of his heart could be felt through the ground like the vibrations of a jackhammer. Porter would stop talking, place his hand against the tree and *feel* where Joe was. Any second now, the man would drop right in front of him, kneel down and say something stupid like "Gotcha now." Then shove his gun right in Joe's face and empty the magazine, splattering his brain all over the underside of the dead oak.

"Yeah, not in the dark," Porter said. After a long pause, he said. "Fine. I'm heading back now."

Joe felt as much as heard a thump from above, then footsteps walking away. It's a trick.

Porter knows where he is. It's all a ploy to get him to reveal himself.

Joe didn't care. He couldn't spend another second underneath that tree. He shimmied out, head first, and waited for the bullet that would finally put an end to the most horrible night of his life.

Chapter 24

Minutes later, Joe rested with his back against the dead oak that had saved his life. Porter didn't materialize out of thin air and kill him. No final bullet punched its way through his skull.

He leaned heavily on the tree and drew deep breaths, slower and slower. His heart finally calming to an almost normal rhythm.

As he sat there, head tilted back, he stared up into the night, letting his mind drift. Through the trees he could see a brilliant field of stars, twinkling, distant. There was no fear up there, so far away.

He recalled a time when he was a boy, no more than fourteen years old. He and his friends had gone camping at the conservation lake. Late in the night, with tents up and the four of them sprawled around the fire, staring up at the sky, one of them, maybe Billy King, had asked, *"How cool would it be to go up there and be the first person to discover aliens?"*

"Oh, that would be awesome!" Paulie had said.

"For real! Maybe they would have blue skin, and four arms," Johnny Dillman had offered.

Joe had said, "Oh, and big eyes, like those manga cartoons!"

"And really big boobs!" Paulie had popped off.

They had agreed, laughing and talking for hours about big alien eyes and big alien boobs. The question of the night becoming "Would you do it with a hot alien with four arms?" They had all agreed, of course they would.

Right then Joe wished for that simpler moment. He wished he were with friends, gazing up at the stars, goofing off, chatting about strange alien life.

Instead of the freedom of the stars and the joy of friends, Joe forced his thoughts back to the real world, one of fear and anger, hatred and terror. He had just killed another man, one who had been trying to kill him. All because he'd tried to help someone.

Though he hurt nearly everywhere at this point, Joe's shoulder still burned from the gun shot. He placed a hand over it, the pain awful and nauseating. Blood still leaked freely from the two holes the bullet had left in the meat of his shoulder. He lifted his arm slowly, testing the movement.

Joe was no doctor, but he was confident that if the bullet had hit bone, he would be in far worse pain than he was now. So, the bullet was a through-and-through, bad, but could be worse. He ripped a length of cloth from the bottom of his shirt and tied it awkwardly around the wound, binding it tightly to stop the bleeding.

With that done, Joe stood and looked back the way he had come and the direction he was sure Porter had left. His hands were covered in grit-caked blood that was growing tacky on his skin. Some of it was his own and some belonged to the dead kidnapper.

Now what, Joe? He thought. They would be expecting him for sure, now, watching every window, patrolling the house. Even if they thought he wouldn't be coming back, Joe knew they would be on high alert until he was dead, or they were gone.

Joe wanted to run. Head into the night and run. Find a farmhouse, a phone. Get help. No matter what he did, he was certain that he wouldn't be able to get to Cady Lynn to protect her before Peavey got to her. Because of all the trouble Joe had caused, he was positive that Peavey would go after Cady Lynn, as payback, even if he were to walk up and give himself over to Peavey's wrath.

Standing there in the dimly lit woods, thinking of his daughter, Joe imagined he heard her scream, far in the distance. Then the scream came again, louder this time, back from the direction of the house.

His shoulders sagged at that scream. He felt it like a cold needle in his heart. Joe cast another glance at the sky, at the twinkling stars and bright moon, wishing silently once more that this was just a terrible dream that he could wake from, right now. He took a reluctant step, then another. He was moving back through the dark woods, back toward the house.

It wasn't *his* daughter screaming, but it was *someone's* daughter.

Chapter 25

"Any asshole with half a brain can go all Rambo and hide in the woods, stabbing people and shit, Peavey. This Pruitt guy has been damn lucky, but sending us all out there, in the dark, chasing after him in the woods is a bad idea. With just the five of us we can hold him off this place for as long as we need to."

Peavey kicked a chair across the kitchen, watching as it skidded across the floor, slammed into a countertop and crashed over on its side. "Bullshit, Aikman! You're saying we let this nobody asshole trap us in the house?"

"No, I'm saying we wait him out 'til morning, when he can't hide anymore. We can see him coming. Then we load up the girls and get the hell out of here."

Peavey waved his arm in the direction of the dark room full of captive girls. "We've got over three million dollars' worth of skin in there because of the special-order girls, where the hell are we going to go? We're still two days out from the hand off, and if we just show up in Chicago, Bolinger will kill every one of us. You don't screw with that woman's plans, and you know it."

Peavey watched as Aikman thought it over.

"Besides, what if this guy stops playing hero and decides to just call the cops? You know who's taking money and who's not. We can't buy 'em all. Just one good cop and were drowning in shit creek."

"That's another thing," Aikman said, "why *hasn't* he called the cops?"

Both men turned when they heard a door open. Seconds later, Porter walked into the kitchen. He bore tiny scratches on his hands and faces from running through the trees. Peavey held up a hand, signaling to the big man that he should wait.

"The only thing I can think of is the Sheriff showing up earlier tonight spooked him. He had to have seen it. Probably doesn't trust anyone at this point."

"Well, let's hope we have that working in our favor, then," Aikman said as he rubbed his hands across his face.

Peavey walked across the room, righted the fallen chair and placed it back at the table. He sat down but quickly stood back up, his face creased and angry. "Yeah, but even if that's the case, it's not something we can count on forever. Eventually he's going to just take the risk and call *somebody*, even if it isn't the local cops or the sheriff."

Porter interjected, "This guy's nuts, I know that. I saw Glenn popping shots at him, and the dude just charged him with a stick, screaming like a damn lunatic. He speared Glenn right in the neck while screaming in his face."

Peavey took two steps toward Porter, glaring at him. "And why didn't you shoot the son-of-bitch if you saw all this!?"

Porter had never worked with Peavey, but

he'd seen what happened to Mike and Dave's faces when the man got angry. He didn't even consider killing him. Bollinger, maybe even Aikman, would bury him if he did. "It was dark, I was too far away, and they were moving around. There was no shot." He didn't mention getting off a shot that actually went through Glenn's head instead of the other guy's.

"Damn it!" Peavey roared. He kicked the chair again, sending it under the table on its back. "Do we have anything to use against the guy? Anything at all?"

Standing at the table, he spun the laptop, so he could see the screen. Aikman had left all of Joe's information up, and Peavey glanced through it all again, thinking. Then he stood ramrod straight and said, "Bring me a girl. Grab the one that's most awake and meet me at the back door. If Joe Pruitt wants to be a hero, lets give him some motivation."

Two minutes later, Peavey stood next to a girl, about thirteen years old, long brown hair, dark circles surrounding her blue eyes. She was thin, athletic looking, wearing track pants and a tank top. She had only just begun to develop into a woman.

The girl was a special order, so he reminded himself to be careful with her. They didn't have time to locate another one if he were to mark her up.

Standing in the full bright light of the lit bulb over the back door, Peavey placed his hand on the girl's neck, squeezing gently to remind her who was in control, and said, "Scream."

The girl, her eyes cloudy and dazed, muttered, "What?"

"Scream. I want you to scream. Loud."

The dark-haired girl stuttered, tears already beginning to leak from the corners of her eyes. "I don't...what...I...I..."

With his face pressed against her cheek, his right eye even with her left, he shouted, "SCREAM!"

The girl tilted her head back and screamed, loud and high.

Peavey reached into his pocket and pulled out a knife. He flicked it open and showed the blade to the girl. He used the fine edge to scrape a line of tears from her face and said, "You scream, really scream, girl, or I'll slice your fucking face off and mail it back to your parents."

Her eyes grew wide, terrified. The last of the drugs they used to keep the girls docile were burned from her system by raw terror. She screamed.

This time, the men standing next to her took a half-step back, hands coming up to cover their ears. Peavey grinned.

The girl stopped, took a deep breath, and screamed once more.

"Enough," Peavey said. He wrapped an arm around her shoulder and pulled her tight to his side. He held the knife up, near her throat, though careful to keep it far enough away so that he wouldn't risk nicking her smooth skin. He couldn't chance devaluing the merchandise.

Lifting his voice, Peavey shouted into the night. "Joe! Mr. Average Joe Pruitt! Are you listening, Joe!? Can you see!?

Peavey waited several minutes, giving Joe plenty of time to get a position in the woods, then he said, "Listen up, Joe, because you need to understand!"

Chapter 26

Joe hunkered down in the tree-line, staying deep in the shadows. He could see the light from the back door of the house, nearly one-hundred yards from where he now squatted in the bushes, across a wide low-cut lawn.

He couldn't make out any detail, but it was obvious that a man stood next to a shorter person, most likely the girl that had been screaming only minutes ago.

From the house, "Listen up Joe, because you need to understand!"

"I understand you're a piece of shit," he muttered into bushes.

"There's nothing you can do to help this girl, Joe! None of them! You've got to understand that!"

Listening, Joe forgot about his own pains for a second. He slapped at a leaf tickling his face with his right hand and hissed at the resurgence of pain in his shoulder. The tunnel of flesh created by the bullet burned fiercely, and he clapped his left hand over it again, pressing firmly.

"Joe, we've been doing this a long time! We're not just going to let a nobody like you walk in and screw it all up! Why don't you just come inside? I promise none of my people will harm you! Let's talk, Joe! I've got a pile of cash sitting here! I'm sure we can negotiate something!"

Joe didn't even consider it, not even for the space of a heartbeat. No money on earth could entice him into that house, or even to simply walk away and let these people continue doing what they were doing. He saw it as an obvious ploy and knew that he would be dead as soon as he showed his face.

He stayed silent, letting Peavey shout to the night air. He may not be a trained soldier, but he wasn't about to respond and give his position away.

Peavey fell silent for a full minute as if he thought Joe might actually reply.

"Fine, Joe! Make it difficult! I know that Anne may be your ex-wife now, but she is still the mother of your child! You'd hate for something to happen to her! I'll make sure it does, Joe. Hell, I might even do it myself. It'll be long and slow, everything bad dreams are made of!"

Joe felt his face flush with anger at the confirmation of his worst thoughts. Peavey would go after Anne and Cady Lynn.

"And Joe, understand one more thing! If you don't come in now, right friggin' NOW, I'll make sure that the men I sell little Cady to are the worst of the worst. The kind that leave nothing but unrecognizable bodies by the time they finish with a girl! Do you hear me Joe Pruitt!? Mr. Average Asshole Joe! Do you fucking hear me!?" The wild, high shouting was just further proof that Peavey was insane, or damn close to it.

Joe felt sick. Deep down sick. Deeper than just in his guts, or even his heart. He felt sick in his soul. He knew, right then, that Peavey would keep his word. He would do just what he said, to Anne, to Cady Lynn. Except now, it didn't matter what Joe did. He could walk up there right now, turn himself over to fate and let Peavey have his way.

Joe would die. Right there. No more talking, no more asking questions of him. Peavey would simply shoot him, or beat him, or have one of the others kill him.

Then he would go after Anne and Cady Lynn. There would be retribution, whether Joe was dead or alive.

Joe understood all of this in a second. He stood up in the bushes, looking at the house, watching the silhouettes there in the light of the porch.

Then he turned and slowly made his way back into the trees.

He wanted to talk to Peavey.

He needed a phone to do that.

Chapter 27

Joe had always enjoyed spending time in the woods. Whether he was with friends camping, even in his youth, or as he got older. He would often prefer the simplicity and comfort that a quiet wood could bring, sometimes just walking. More than once, he had gone out under the trees far from people and simply sat down beneath a broad oak or stately sycamore and fell asleep.

Now, walking through these dark woods, the many tiny cuts and scratches from leaves and branches were an annoyance, and he felt no comfort, only a slow, persistent fear. The anticipation of a surprise attack out of the night by Peavey or one of his men was a constant weight on his mind.

Carefully picking his path through the dark undergrowth, Joe found his way back to the body of the man he had speared in the throat. He circled the corpse several times, wondering if his fellow kidnappers would return for the body, or if he meant so little to them that they would just leave him out here to rot or be eaten by wildlife. They would most likely collect the body before leaving. Peavey or Aikman would be unwilling to risk a lone hunter with his dog finding it and calling the cops.

Flies had already begun to collect around the corpse, drawn, Joe imagined, by the hot-penny smell of blood and the reek of feces wafting off the body with the faint breeze. *I hope he didn't* carry his phone in his back pocket, Joe thought.

Joe stopped circling and squatted down next to the dead man, avoiding the lake of blood now soaking into the ground around the corpse. The man had been wearing a white tee shirt, now soaked down the front like a bloody bib. His dark jeans blended into the night and the ground.

Reaching out with his left hand, his right arm laying across his knees, Joe patted the front of the man's pants, jerking his hand away at first when he found them to be soaking wet. He held his hand up to the moonlight, relieved to find no blood. The man's bodily functions had released when he died. A faint, sardonic smile lifted the corners of Joe's mouth. He liked the idea of the big bad kidnapper pissing and shitting himself when he died. It seemed like a fitting final indignity.

He found nothing in the front pockets and groaned. Instead of giving himself over to thoughts of the unpleasant task, Joe quickly reached underneath the man and felt the left pants pocket. He found nothing there but cold dampness.

He chose not to roll the body, and stood, walking around and squatting at the other side. He pushed his hand underneath the man's rear and still felt nothing.

Joe spat a curse, and stood, thinking. Then he remembered that the man had been shining a light in his face as he was popping off shots with his other hand. If Porter hadn't found the phone and taken it with him, it should be lying on the ground somewhere nearby.

For a full minute, Joe listened to the sound of the woods around him, turning to get every angle. He heard nothing other than light soughing of the wind and the normal animal and insect sounds of a nighttime forest.

No one was approaching, at least not that he could tell. Moving slowly, Joe began to shuffle his way around the body, barely picking up his feet. The noise he was making made him distinctly uncomfortable, but finding a cell phone in the dark, on the ground, possibly under the leaves, wasn't something he felt like doing on his hands and knees, especially with the way his right shoulder was hurting.

His mind wandered while he searched, and he found himself wishing for a handful of ibuprofen or aspirin, something to dull the edge of pain in his shoulder, along with the pain in his face and side. Too many different points of pain. He thought about swallowing the pills with a cold beer, the smooth taste, the cold hitting the back of his throat. A sandwich would be nice, or another burger, or roast beef piled high on some rye bread, slathered with a thick layer of horseradish sauce and some swiss cheese.

It had been hours since he had eaten. He didn't realize how hungry he really was. Even the presence of a dead man, one that he himself had killed, seemed incapable of dulling his appetite.

Every few shuffled steps, he would be pulled from his thoughts when the toe of his shoe struck something hard. Usually a stick, but he also found two rocks, and something that looked like a walnut. He bent again and reached in front of his foot, expecting another stone or stick, when his fingers wrapped around something with straight edges.

He lifted the phone up, with a whispered, "Yes!" and pressed a button on the side, bringing it to life. He had been in the dark so long that the sudden light stung his eyes. He had to squint for a moment to even see the screen. It was unlocked. There were no personal pictures, just a swirl of colors. The default setting for the phone, he imagined. He swiped it away and looked at the service icon. Two bars for service, and a weak internet connection via 4g.

Joe took the phone and went around the large oak he had hidden behind earlier, using the light from the screen as a guide. He didn't want to turn on the bright flashlight.

Once he was behind the tree, he took a moment to adjust the screen brightness to its lowest setting and changed the screen timeout to five seconds. He also muted the ringer, so that Peavey wouldn't be able to call the phone and discover his location. He was glad to see that the battery was at 62% charge. He had some time, though he had no idea how long Peavey would wait before frustration set in and he sent men after him again.

Joe sat there behind the tree, just looking at the phone. The screen went dark as he thought about calling Paul again, let him know he was still alive. He also considered calling Anne, maybe warn her to be on the lookout for some bad men who wanted to hurt her and Cady Lynn. Neither call would do him any good. Joe understood that what he really wanted was the comfort of a friendly voice and not someone who was hellbent on killing him.

Joe pulled in a deep breath and slowly let it out. He pushed aside all other thoughts, brought the screen back to life and tapped the browser icon. He would call Peavey soon, but first he wanted some information.

After several minutes of tapping, searching and waiting for slow web pages to load, Joe knew the location of the closest regional FBI offices. He saved their phone numbers in the phone. He did the same for the sheriff's office and two different police departments. Then, he found the numbers for several TV and radio news stations. He saved those as well.

He wasn't sure *how* he would use them, but he felt better for having them.

Joe was now ready to make the call he dreaded.

Chapter 28

Peavey came back through the door and shoved the girl toward Scales. The tattooed man caught the stumbling captive and walked her back to the room where the others were being kept. To Aikman, Porter and Nate he said, "Keep a close watch. I would say I expect him to show up any minute now, willing to do anything to protect his daughter, but this jackass has been unpredictable from the get-go. If he actually comes in, great, I can end this shit. If not, we'll just have to hunt his ass down."

"Yeah, because that's been working out well, so far." Aikman glared at Peavey. "You just had to bring this shit to my door, didn't you? I think it's about time we call Bolinger and let her know what the hell is going on out here."

Peavey stormed across the room, his face darkening. "Screw you, Aikman! How many years have we been doing this? This is some fluke bullshit, is what it is. We'll fix it. Don't you even think about calling Bolinger," Peavey shoved a finger in Aikman's face, the tip of his trimmed fingernail centimeters from the man's nose. "She's the last thing any of us need."

"So, what if he doesn't come in, then what?"

Peavey scrubbed his hands over the top of his head, leaving his hair a wild mop. "Hell, I don't know. Maybe we can send those three out to run him down, force him to come this way. We can't let some nobody asshole trap us here in the house, Aikman. We run this show, and he needs to know that. Right before I put a bullet in his fucking head!" Spittle flew as Peavey spoke, his face growing redder with every word.

Peavey stormed around the kitchen, out into the living area of the old farmhouse, then back into the kitchen. He stopped in the doorway between rooms braced his hands on both sides of the door as if he were trying to bring the house down like Samson. He glanced at his watch. It was almost one o'clock in the morning.

"Shit. Okay, if we don't have this guy by five, we'll call Bolinger. I'd rather tell her about it afterwards then have her send people down here herself. Or, God forbid, she comes down. Jesus, that'd be a real shit-show."

Aikman nodded and went to sit at the table again, pulling the laptop close, tapping for a moment at the keys.

"What're you doing?" Peavey asked.

Aikman didn't look up from the computer as he said, "Research."

Peavey stormed away, walking from room to room, window to window. He checked with each of the men, asking if they had seen anything, knowing full well if they had he wouldn't have to ask. It was movement, doing *some*thing, because he hated sitting in the house just waiting for Joe to make his next move.

Back in the kitchen, he sat down at the table and watched as Aikman banged away at the keyboard. "Easy on my computer. I've got a lot of important shit on there."

Aikman responded with a nod.

Peavey scrubbed his hands on his pant legs, fiddled with his jacket, pulled at his collar. He stood, walked to the sink, walked to the fridge, stumped back to the table, went back to the refrigerator, opened it, grabbed a bottle of water, went back to the table, sat down.

"Peavey, you're…" Aikman began. He was cut off when Peavey's phone chimed in his pocket. He dug it out and looked at the screen. It was Glenn's phone. "Did you give Glenn my number?"

"I gave all the guys your number, right after you got here, just in case. Why?"

"Glenn's calling me." Peavey sat up straight in the chair, his mouth pulling into a tight line. "Get in here!" he shouted. The other three men ran into the room and Peavey said, "He's calling me on Glenn's phone, get outside and watch for him, he might be close! If you see him, kill the bastard!"

Peavey pressed his finger against the flashing green icon and swiped. He lifted the phone to his ear and said, "Hello, Joe, whadda ya know?"

"Hello, Peavey. I know you're a piece of shit. Let's talk."

Chapter 29

Joe pressed himself close the ground, with the phone held to his ear. He could watch the house through the bush he was under, at an angle that allowed him to see if anyone came around it and into the woods. His right shoulder protested the awkward position he was laying in, and he did his best to ignore it.

"Hello, Joe, whadda ya know?"

"Hello, Peavey. I know you're a piece of shit. Let's talk." He kept his voice low, almost a whisper.

"You don't know anything about me, Mr. Average Joe. Not a damn thing. But you will. Me, on the other hand, well, I know a lot about you. The internet is a wonderful tool, don't you think?"

"I know enough, Peavey. More than I ever cared to know. I know you kidnap young girls and sell them. That by itself is all anyone needs to know, and Peavey, I'm gonna make sure the whole world knows."

The smell of rich dirt and decomposing leaves filled his sinuses. At one time, it was a scent Joe was fond of, now, at this moment, it was almost cloying, as if simply being in the proximity of men like Peavey tainted the world, turning everything into the stench of vile rot.

"Joe, this is just business. Where there's a demand, there must be a supply. I fill that supply. Me, and many more just like me."

"Human trafficking isn't *'just business'* Peavey. It's sick. You're sick." Joe paused, taking a shallow breath. Three men came out of the house, spreading out and watching the tree-line. "Just so you know, I've got a message all ready to send to the FBI, and every news station I could find. If your boys take one step into these woods, I'm hanging up and hitting send on it."

A garbled shout came from the house and the men, who were merely darker shadows in the night, stopped moving.

"Fine, Joe. Let's talk then."

Peavey's voice was calm and conversational, but Joe could detect a hint of tension, as if the man were fighting to keep his composure. Good, he thought. Joe opened his mouth to speak, then immediately closed it, realizing that he had no idea what he was going to say.

Silence held the line, neither man speaking. Dead air, filled only with the sounds of breathing.

After nearly a full minute, Peavey, his voice taking on a taunting lilt, said, *"Joe, what're you doing? You're so far out of your league here. Yeah, you've gotten lucky, but don't let it go to your head. Come in, the guys will let you through, and we can talk, man to man."*

Joe rested his head on the ground, inhaling the heady loam smell for several deep breaths and said, "You're no man. None of you are. You're sick. Anyone who would do what you people do is sick. Just let the girls go. Let them go and…"

"And what, Joe? You'll trade your life for theirs, maybe? Are you really that noble? Are you truly that brave, Joe Pruitt? That…stupid?"

"Screw you, Peavy. I may be nobody, but I'm damn sure not just gonna let you have those girls."

"Of course you're not, Mr. Average Joe. I already have them, and there's nothing you can do about it. You're tapped out. I can hear it in your voice. You've got nothing left. Eventually, you'll fuck up and I'll put you down, Joe. And I'll still have the girls. You'll be a rotting corpse, pieces of you in various states, and these girls, well, they'll travel too, maybe some will even see other places, beyond our borders. Well, at least while they're useful.

The condescending tone in Peavey's voice became more pronounced with every word. Joe was being taunted and he knew it. He still couldn't help the intense rage he felt at the man's oily voice. Every word seemed to seep into the fine runnels of his brain and poison his thoughts.

"I might… I, I… maybe…I, I'm not as easy to kill as you think," Joe stammered. He knew his utter lack of confidence had come through in every word.

On the other end of the line, Peavey laughed. Joe could almost picture his head tilting back, his face breaking into a wide-open grin. Something alien, ready to consume its prey, cackling out joyfully over its kill.

"Joe, you just don't get it. Just a few of

these girls, in this house, right now, will bring a couple million dollars. The ones special-ordered by our clients. Hell, a regular snatch-and-grab like you witnessed can be worth ten to fifteen grand, Pruitt. Sometimes much, much more, depending on the buyer and what they intend to do with her. Some of these guys will easily pay a hundred-thousand for a girl they're only going to use for a night or two. You really *don't want to know* how *they use them, I can promise you that."*

It was obvious to Joe that Peavey was enjoying this bit of verbal theatrics. As much as he hated to admit it, it was getting to him. He could feel that tight knot forming in his stomach again as brutal, bloody images of used and broken girls flashed through his mind. Girls disappeared all the time on the streets of America and were never seen again.

"Piss off, Peavey, you sick shit! You...you...you're done! I'm gonna make sure of it! You're done!" Joe had to fight to keep his voice down, hating the weak sound of his own stammered words.

Laughing again, Peavey ignored the threat. *"This is a big money game, Joe. One you're not prepared to play."*

Laying in the dark, under a bush, Joe wasn't sure why ever wanted to talk to Peavey. It was a futile effort, nothing would be gained by it. It had only served to embolden the kidnapper and to remind Joe just how inadequate he really was.

Joe pulled the phone away from his ear

when Peavey shouted on the other end. As he watched, the men who had stood eyeing the dark woods now turned, their shadows quickly disappearing behind the house and they were gone.

"Ok, Joe. No more screwing around. I've called the men back. You have a free pass to walk on into this house and you and I can work something out. This is my last offer. Take it, Joe. Now. Let's put an end to this silly bullshit. You know as well as I do that you're incapable of rescuing these girls. Or Cady."

Joe pulled the phone away from his face and looked at the dim screen. His hand was shaking when he flicked out a finger to tap the red end icon. Seconds later the screen went dark and Joe still stared at it, his face pulled together in a tight, angry scowl.

He knew he couldn't walk away, trained mercenary, skilled killer or not. It didn't matter now. He had to stop Peavey and the others.

Chapter 30

"Keep watching the windows, but don't go back outside, at least not for a while. Let him get comfortable, let his guard down. He's got some hero complex. Thinks he's going to rescue the girls and ride off into the sunset. Eventually good ol' Joe is gonna have to come to the house, either to try and talk this out or push some sort of assault on us. Regardless, we'll have him then and can put an end to this shit."

The other men looked at Peavey, watching his agitated pacing as he spoke. When he stopped speaking, all but Aikman went to find a window watching the woods near the house.

"Peavey, we need to call Bolinger, let her know what the hell is going on. If you're not at the other house when they come for pickup, she'll be pissed."

"We've got two days before pickup, and we'll let her know once we've handled this. We can do the hand-off here just as easily as back there."

Peavey stopped pacing and sat down at the table.

"Fine, you're the boss. For the record, I don't like it." Aikman's phone chimed in his pocket and he slipped it out, tapping the screen. He began to thumb a message.

Peavey glanced from the phone to Aikman's face and back, perturbed. "Who the hell is that? You better not be talking to Bolinger, damn it."

He began to stand up from the table.

"Jesus man, chill out. It's my sister, well, my sister's husband."

"Why would your sister's husband be messaging you this late at night?'

"She just had a kid, Peavey. Like, an hour ago. Seriously man, you've got to relax. This Pruitt guy has you all messed up."

Peavey considered snatching the phone from Aikman, reading the messages. He sat back down, rubbed at his face and adjusted the pistol in its holster under his left arm.

"Yeah... yeah."

Aikman turned and walked from the room, still tapping at the phone. Peavey shouted, "And for your information, you don't have to like it!"

Peavey wore his frustration on his face. He hadn't slept in almost day and he was beginning to feel it. He had never had a problem like this, ever, not on any grab, or any hand-off. People had tried to double-cross him, filch on the money they owed, little things he handled easily, usually with a bullet. Now, one guy had thrown everything into utter chaos.

Chapter 31

Joe backed into the woods and stood watching the dark silhouette of the house, frustrated that he couldn't just run-and-gun his way up there and rescue the girls. Angry that he had no plan, or even a nugget of a plan, to build on.

He couldn't just assault the house. He'd be dead within seconds. He didn't know if the three men who had come out when he was on the phone with Peavey were the only ones he had left, or if there were more waiting inside, so sneaking up, freeing the girls and running into the woods with them was completely out of the question. Besides, they were all probably so drugged that they wouldn't be able to run even if he *could* set them free.

Thinking about the men, Joe realized he hadn't seen another vehicle anywhere. Not the white van Peavey, Mike, and Dave had used to bring the girls here. He figured that Aikman and his crew must have a van of their own, and possibly a secondary vehicle, just as Peavey's crew had.

Then where the hell were they? There was no attached garage, and Joe had seen both the front and back of the house. He assumed they could be parked along the far side, away from him, overshadowed by the house but working on assumption made him nervous. He had to know where their vehicles were.

With a faint twinge of hope, Joe began moving along the tree-line, staying well within the shadows and circling behind the house.

The house was outlined by the bright moon, and as he made his way further around, he could see there were no vehicles parked on the far side.

That little bit of hope Joe felt started to diminish, only to be rekindled several minutes later when a broad, dim shape began to appear in the darkness to right of the house. From his angle it looked to be only a couple of yards from the trees. As he got closer and the shape resolved in the night, he could see that it was an old barn.

He pushed on through the woods, moving quicker, though still conscious of the noise he was making. Joe had seen no one come from the house and prayed that he wasn't loud enough to be heard inside, even though every scrape of leaves and scuffle of foot seemed to be a clarion call to the kidnappers, as loud as a klaxon blaring his position in the trees.

Minutes later Joe was standing at the edge of the woods, watching the structure, thinking. Would they have placed a guard inside, or had they been confident enough to leave the vehicles unattended?

The barn was a third the size of the house, squat and spread out. Its dark shape was like a hunkering beast, sleeping. Joe watched, waited and listened. Ten minutes later, he stepped out of the woods directly behind the barn. He couldn't see the house, which meant no one inside the house could see him.

Hunching down and keeping his profile as low as possible, Joe darted across the two yards of grass that separated the trees from the barn. Pressing his back against the rough old wood, and laying his ear against the back wall, he listened. Nothing, no sound at all.

With his heart climbing toward his throat, Joe sidled along the blank back wall of the barn and peeked around the corner. Along the side was a single window, set half-way down, though it looked to be boarded up.

He could also see the house, and the one window on this side. Light spilled from it, illuminating the patch of grass around it for several feet.

He ducked back behind the barn and went the other direction. At the far end, he peeked around again, and then took a step out, away from the building. This side of the barn was also just yards from the woods, which were cut into an L shape. The trees ran both ways, creating a tidy corner. The grass was high here, almost to his knees. It was a place often overlooked by whoever cared for the grounds.

Moving cautiously, remembering that he had yet to verify for certain that the barn was unguarded, Joe moved up to the front corner, pressed his back against the wall several feet from the end, and sidled down. Once at the edge, he glanced around the corner once, quickly, giving himself only a second to survey the area in front of the barn. He did it once more, and then a third time. When he was satisfied no one was standing at the doors, he peeked around and watched for a full minute.

The area in front of the barn was the same gravel as the driveway, which led from the doors of the barn, across the front of the house, and curving up to create the lane to the gate. The trees here angled out and then back up, following the drive. He was unable to see the gate or the truck he had left jammed against it.

Joe could see why the kidnappers had chosen this property. The long drive from the gate to the house, the only thing visible of the property from the road was a small section of the house itself and the gate. Everything else was concealed by the thick screen of woods around the entire property.

Joe could imagine that at one time this land was entirely covered in trees, and that the original owner had cleared it be this perfect isolated spot, a place to live away from the world, while still being part of it. It was something Joe himself had dreamed of many times over the years.

He continued watching the house for another minute before pulling back and walking freely down the side of the barn to the boarded window. Using the dead man's phone and holding it close to the side of the barn, he pressed the button to bring it to life, and swiped open the main screen. The dim light showed him two things. The wood over the windows was new, store bought; it was not old, washed out and rough like the barn wall around it. And they were screwed in, not nailed.

The screen went black and he slipped it into his left-hand jacket pocket. The right still held the pistol.

He teased his fingers underneath the edge of the bottom board, his right shoulder protesting the movement with a spark of pain, and attempted to pull it away from the wall. The board didn't move. "Shit," he muttered, and tried again. Nothing.

He thought that if he had a pry bar or some other tool, he might be able to pop the boards loose, but because they were screwed in and not nailed, it would probably make enough noise to alert anyone in the house to his location.

Joe placed his forehead against the rough boards and sighed. His only options were to somehow tear his way through the window or wall in complete silence, or slip around the front, open the door to the garage and walk inside.

Joe moved toward the front of the building again and eyed the house. He stood that way for five minutes, watching. He decided that if he wanted inside the garage, he would have to take the risk.

Staying low, Joe slipped around the corner and slid with his back along the wall and his left hand out guiding him, feeling for the edge of the door. His eyes scanning the house and surrounding yard the entire time.

The doors were split down the middle and would swing wide in opposite directions if they were opened at the same time, allowing entry of vehicles. There was no man-size door. When he reached the middle of the doors, Joe saw a hasp and padlock, and his heart sank to his stomach.

He reached out and carefully grasped the heavy padlock, and pulled. The lock twisted in his hand, shifting. It hadn't been latched, only hung in place to appear as if it were locked.

He guessed that the men would want a quick and easy exit, should they have to leave in a hurry. Getting a key out, into a lock, and opening the door may take more time than it was worth. When they were gone from the house all at once was probably the only time the lock was secured.

With a gentle grip, Joe pulled the shank up through the loop of the staple and swung the hasp open. He re-hooked the shank, leaving the lock dangling. He hoped that when the door was pulled closed, it would appear, at least at a cursory glance, that the latch was undisturbed. Joe's eyes flicked back and forth between the lock and the house the entire time he spent removing and replacing the lock.

Still no movement from the house, no one watching from the window. He hoped they were focusing on the other side, his last known position. Still crouched, Joe tugged open the door, cringing at the rough grating of the hinges. With the door open just far enough to slip inside, between the closed half and the side he held, he poked his head in, drew it back out quickly, glanced back at the house, then pushed between the door halves and closed it behind him. He barely heard the faint clink of the hasp tapping against the hanging padlock.

Crouched inside the pitch-dark barn, with the door closed at his back, Joe went to one knee and released the breath he hadn't realized he had been holding.

With something solid between himself and the kidnappers, Joe felt a sense of relief. For the first time in hours, he couldn't be easily spotted by a lucky observer. However, he now also had no view of the house and the men inside.

Crouching there in the darkness, Joe was suddenly overwhelmed with the idea that Peavey had known Joe would find the barn, that he had been watching all along, waiting for Joe to trap himself like a rat in a cage. He could *feel* Peavey and his men creeping up outside the doors, ready to toss them wide and put him down with a volley of gunfire.

His heart began to slam in his chest, and he considered opening the door and slipping back out, into the night, and running for the woods.

Joe took several deep breaths and lay down on the dirt floor, pressing his face to the ground and an eye to the gap under the door. Nothing. No feet attached to men waiting to ambush him. A glint of light from the house and nothing else.

Joe moved back into a crouch, then stood, slowly. He couldn't entirely shake the idea that Peavey and his men were coming for him, that they somehow knew exactly where he was.

Chapter 32

Peavey angled through the kitchen and looked around the doorway that Aikman had gone through. He watched the man tapping at the phone screen, his scowl deepening. He stepped through the door, walking directly toward Aikman. "Still talking to your brother-in-law?"

Aikman looked up from the device and backed up a step at Peavey's approach. "Huh? Oh, yeah. He's pretty excited, ya know? New baby and all."

Peavey enjoyed the shocked look on Aikman's face when he reached out and snatched the phone from his hands, even as Aikman was attempting to turn away from him.

"What the hell, Peavey!?"

"Hey, I just wanna see the baby pics," he said with a dark grin. The screen hadn't gone black yet and he tapped the message icon, then the most recent message.

"Her flight landed over an hour ago. She'll be here in about half an hour," Aikman said.

Looking up from the phone, glaring at Aikman, Peavey said, "Yeah, I can see that. When did you talk to her?"

"Right after you got here. When you told me what happened, I thought she should know. I knew you wouldn't tell her."

"Damn right I wasn't going to tell her, not until *after* it was fixed."

Aikman backed away when Peavey took a

step towards him, his lips pulling tight. Peavey knew the man was waiting to get hit. That would only complicate things later, with Bolinger.

Peavey reached out and took Aikman's left hand. Aikman flinched and tried to pull away, then Peavey slapped the phone back into the man's hand. "Let me know when she's here," he spat. He turned away and stalked out of the room.

Chapter 33

Joe tugged the phone from his pocket and brought the screen to life. Using only the dim light from the screen, he began to search the barn.

The first vehicle was only a foot away, and he quickly identified it as the white van from the previous day. The dried spatters of his own vomit were still on the back door.

He bypassed that and moved forward, deeper into the darkness. In front of the white van, sat another just like it, almost identical, except it had no smear of sick on the door. To the left of the second van sat a car under a car cover. Moving to the back he lifted the cover and realized it was a car that, under normal circumstances, he would have given an appreciative whistle for. Though he couldn't see much with the meager light from the phone, he could tell it was a restored Camaro, probably a '67 or '68. The dark green paint seemed to shimmer under the faint light. He tugged the cover back in place.

Now that's a getaway car, he thought. He could imagine the roar and rumble when the road-beast started up. Joe had always wanted to restore an older car like this one, something that was all muscle and speed just waiting to be unleashed.

He made a circuit of the vehicles, which filled most of the space in the low barn. Along the left wall, near the Camaro, there was a rack of tools that could be found in most any country home's shed. Hammers and saws, files and screwdrivers, a double-bladed axe and heavy splitting maul, shovels, rakes, a spading fork, and more. He even found a small chainsaw on the shelf under a narrow workbench.

He tried to push out the boards of the window on the side away from the house, thinking they might come free from inside more easily than they would from out, but they were firmly screwed into place. Not a single centimeter of give.

Joe hadn't known what he would find inside the barn, but the lawn and garden tools left him feeling frustrated. Nothing there would be of any use to him. He moved over to the front van, the one he had never been in and reached for the door handle. Joe stopped himself before opening it, realizing that the light inside would come on the moment he opened the door.

The windows were sealed up tightly, but light might still shine through cracks, and the gap under the door was wide enough to slide a hand under. Any light from inside would surely be visible to anyone who happened to look toward the barn, even if they were in the house.

"Shit," he muttered. Moving back toward the wall of tools and the narrow bench, he looked for something he could use to block out the light. After several minutes of fruitless searching he had found nothing of use.

Joe leaned back against the workbench and

sighed. He let the phone go dark to save the battery. He thumbed it back on seconds later. The blackness seemed to swallow him and, for the first time in his life, Joe felt a gnawing fear of the dark.

The Camaro sat squat and hidden beneath the car cover in front of him, and he wondered what it would be like to ride away in that car. To just throw the cover off, start the car with a roar, and be off, down the road, away from the nightmare of kidnappers and stolen girls.

Joe's eyes flew wide and he took a step forward, toward the car. The cover! He lifted a corner of it again. It was pliable, soft enough to make little noise. Taking care to remove it slowly, Joe slid the cover off the car with one hand, while holding the lit phone in the other.

With the cover free, he bunched it up tightly, holding it close to his body and went back to the large double doors. He let the phone go dark, knelt on the floor, then lay down, pressing his eye to the crack at the bottom. Taking shallow breaths, he watched for a full minute. No movement.

Standing, he lay the car cover on the ground and stretched it out to its full length. Then he pressed it against the base of the doors, careful that none of the heavy cloth pushed out underneath.

After several minutes of fussing with the cover, making sure it was just right, he was satisfied no light would leak out from under the door. With the car cover in place, Joe lay down on the floor once more and shifted an inch of the fabric. With little work he could still see a slice of the house and drive.

Standing at the rear of the first van, with only a foot of space between him and the doors, Joe tapped the flashlight icon on the phone and a wide, bright beam pushed the darkness back. The battery was down to 28%.

Mentally, Joe crossed his fingers and began searching the vehicles for anything he could use.

Chapter 34

Peavey paced through the house, his hands working nervously. Using the fingernail on the index finger of his right hand, he had scraped away a thick layer of dried skin on the edge of his thumbnail. It was beginning to bleed, and he stuck the side of it in his mouth, sucking at the tiny wound.

The last thing he wanted was Bolinger down here. Any time she had to leave Chicago, it didn't turn out well for whoever made her leave. Whether she would see that as Aikman or himself was the unanswered question that made him so twitchy.

He hoped he could convince her that the fault for this lay squarely at the feet of Mike and Dave. If they hadn't gone for the unauthorized snatch-and-grab, none of this would be happening. Also, they were both dead, killed as a result of their own idiotic actions. With any luck, that would dissipate her anger enough that at least he would come out of it with all his digits attached.

Only twice in the six years he had been running girls for Bolinger had he witnessed her personally handle someone who had screwed up. Both times were quick, bloody, and completely unexpected.

The first time had been a runner that had allowed a girl to escape by not securing her properly and failing to keep her doped up.

Peavey had been at her Chicago home by request when the call came in that the kid had escaped. She told him to join her, and they flew down to St. Louis, where they met with the runner.

Bolinger's conversation with the runner had lasted less than two minutes. The man had stammered out an explanation. Bolinger had nodded, said she understood, then the guy's right eye had disappeared at the same time the woman's pistol roared. Peavey couldn't remember ever seeing her reach for the gun. It was simply there, as if produced through some slight-of-hand.

The second time had been a year ago, with one of Peavey's own crew. The man had broken Bolinger's number one solid rule for which there was no forgiveness. Hands off the merchandise. The man, Eckler, had raped one of the girls.

Bolinger had shown up at the holding house in the middle of the night, sat down at the kitchen table, and called for Eckler. Peavey and his other crewmen stood by and watched, at her demand, as she excoriated the man. She had told Eckler to place his hands on the table, as if he were about to be wacked with a ruler for talking out of turn. Again, she proved just how fast her hands were.

Three fingers on Eckler's right hand had disappeared in a splash of blood and a scream. She had cut and swiped them from the table in one smooth move, so fast, that again, it seemed like magic. As the man stood there, holding up his hand, staring at the blood pumping from the bleeding digits, Bolinger had walked around the table, gently placed a hand on his shoulder and rammed the eight-inch blade she was holding into his back.

Bolinger had let Eckler crumple to his knees, the knife still in his back. The glance she shot to the other men had sent a chill down Peavey's arms that raised gooseflesh. Every one of them understood. Hands off.

The girl had been useless after that. Nearly every buyer wanted virgins, or at least clean and unbruised. They had dumped her body off a bridge into fast-moving river a thousand miles from her home.

Bolinger had left the holding house without saying anything to him or anyone else that night. She hadn't needed to.

"Peavey?"

Peavey stopped pacing, pulled the sore thumb away from his mouth and looked at Aikman standing in the doorway between the kitchen and the dining room with his phone in hand.

"She's here."

Chapter 35

Joe sat in the driver side of the front van, pawing through the center console. Papers, gum wrappers, an empty pistol magazine, phone charger cord. A half-melted chocolate bar which he tore open and ate immediately.

He sifted through the trash between the seats and in the footwell of the passenger side. The detritus of a long drive. He found a half-empty bottle of water wedged under the passenger's seat. He twisted the top off and brought the bottle up, stopping just before it touched his lips.

Did he really want to drink from the same container that one of the kidnappers had drunk from? Evil wasn't a contagion like the flu. Joe could easily imagine taking a swig from the bottle and seconds later being ready to walk into the house and join the men in their wicked deeds, as if drinking water contaminated by one of them would infect him and rewrite his thought processes to not only willingly accept, but take part in, the most heinous of crimes.

Joe tipped the bottle up and swallowed the water, his thirst greater than his trepidation at being zombified into a kidnapping criminal. He recapped the bottle and dropped it with the other trash piled on the floor.

In the glove compartment he found a partial box of 9mm ammunition, but no gun to go with it. The pistol he had in his jacket pocket was a .45. He left the bullets there, closed the compartment and slipped into the back of the van, where he found nothing. It was completely empty.

Before crawling out of the van, Joe plugged the stolen phone into the USB jack in the dash with the cord had had found in the center console. With that done, he got out and gently closed the door, pushing until the latch clicked and the interior light blinked out.

He went to the second van, saving the car for last. He had already been in the van previously but didn't have the time to give it a decent search previously. He had been too terrified at the time, worried that he would be found and shot every time he couldn't see above the dash.

Now, he spent several minutes rummaging through the vehicle. He came away with a package of chili-spiced peanuts, another bottle of water, unopened, and nothing else. He considered taking some of the paperwork belonging in the van, like the insurance card or registration in the glove compartment to turn in to authorities later. He left it, after a moment's thought, realizing that he would have to get away alive to hand it over to the anyone, and that if these people had been doing this for a long time, they most likely had covered their tracks well when came to paperwork.

They couldn't risk unanswerable questions if they should happen to get pulled over because one of their people ran a stop sign or got a little too far above the speed limit. Joe could imagine that if the van were empty, the vehicle and its paperwork would easily pass any inspection by a police officer. If the van were full of girls being transported to their next location, Joe could just as easily see the driver of the van shooting a cop and running and dumping the van as soon as they were able to replace it.

With the second van searched, Joe exited, shut the door as carefully as he had the first van's, and moved to the car in the dark. He felt his way along the smooth panels, finding the handle by touch. With the door open and the dome-light on, he sat down in the passenger seat.

The car had a two-tone green interior, every inch of it gleaming and clean. There was no trash piled in the floor. The owner probably never ate or drank anything in the vehicle, and if he did, he took his garbage with him every time he got out.

Joe sank into the bucket seat, allowing himself a moment to just let his body relax. He had been carrying so much tension, his muscles felt as tight as a twisted steel cable. He felt every jab and tingle of pain, and his right shoulder had begun to stiffen up, every movement painful and difficult. He wondered if he went to long without having it looked at by a doctor if the damage to the muscle would irreparable.

He shrugged his shoulders and rolled his head around, wincing at the grating and popping noises. He guessed it wouldn't really matter about his shoulder if he were dead.

Joe sat up straight and focused. It was obvious that he would find nothing, but he felt under the front seats anyway. He was right. Clean. Not even that layer of grit that seemed to collect beneath a car's seat.

He popped open the glove compartment, finding nothing but papers. He took a second and glanced at the name on the registration. Andrew A. Aikman. Triple A. Someone's parents had thought they were being clever. Mr. Aikman probably didn't think so when he was getting picked on and harassed as a boy.

Muttering, Joe said, "Mr. Andrew A. Aikman, you've got great taste in cars. Too bad you're a kidnapping asshole."

Joe tossed the papers back into the compartment and closed it. He turned to give the back seat a cursory glance. It was utterly spotless back there. Had anyone ever sat in that seat?

He climbed out of the car and pressed the door closed. He would have liked to check the trunk, but he couldn't without the key which was probably in Aikman's pocket. Surely never more than an arm's-length away.

Back in the darkness, Joe felt his way to the rear of the car and leaned against the trunk. He smiled at the thought that doing this would probably piss the owner off had he known.

He had gotten a drink and a snack out of the vehicles and nothing more. Other than some basic farm and yard tools, he had found nothing in the barn of any real use. Though he hadn't known what to expect, he had at least hoped there was something he could use to take out Peavey and the others.

Joe felt like time was running out.

Standing there in the darkness, Joe placed his left hand on the back of his neck and squeezed, as if he could tease out a thought by working the tired muscles. Then he heard a voice, distant and muffled by the door. He was sure it was a woman's voice.

"Take a walk around the house, then meet me inside."

Oh God, what now?

As fast as he could in the dark while trying not to stumble or scuff his feet on the dirt floor, Joe made his way to the door and lay down at the far-right corner. He teased away several inches of the cover and pressed his eye to the gap.

He could see two dark shapes approaching the house on foot. The narrow slice of the world the gap afforded him, prevented Joe from making out any detail.

One of the shapes broke away from the other and moved along the side of the house in the direction of the barn. Joe's heart started to pound, then the shape rounded the corner, passed by the lit window along the side of the house he could see and disappeared around the back corner.

At the same time, the other shape walked up to the house, and without knocking or announcing its presence, opened the door and walked in.

Joe felt that raw, sinking feeling in his stomach again. Things had changed, something was happening. The female voice had said,

"Take a walk around the house, then meet me inside." Which meant the second dark shape would be coming back around. Joe waited, watching, taking small breaths.

Two minutes later the dark shape reappeared from the opposite end of the house and moved toward the door. To Joe it looked like whoever it was stopped and looked around once more before stepping through the door and into the house.

Whoever they were, whatever they were doing, Joe was sure it was bad, for him or for the girls, maybe both.

Joe needed to know what was happening inside that house.

Chapter 36

Peavey sat down at the kitchen table, attempting nonchalance. He was there for a second before standing up again and leaning against the countertop next to the double sink. He was about to move again when he heard the front door open, followed by footsteps.

From the front room he heard, "Where's Peavey?"

Aikman's voice replied, "In the kitchen, ma'am."

"Can the "ma'am" shit, Andrew. I'm not in the mood for ass-kissing."

Peavey swallowed. The woman's voice cracked like a whip, and he could already feel the sting of that lash.

The woman stepped into the kitchen, walked directly toward him, stopping a foot away. Peavey's skin crawled at her direct gaze. "What the hell's going on, Anthony?"

Peavey had stood toe-to-toe with some very big men, backing them all down. He had faced off against the police and FBI agents on more than one occasion and walked away without his heartrate ever climbing above normal.

This woman was one of a small, select group that made him genuinely nervous. He began to pick at the sore thumb again and forced himself to stop. Sucking on a bleeding thumb was only going to make him look weak and inept and would only irritate MerylAnn Bolinger even more than she already was.

Standing straight, and looking back as directly as she eyed him, Peavey said, "Meryl, you didn't have to come all the way down here. I'll have it handled soon."

The woman stood no more than five-and-a-half feet tall, her hair dark brown with faint streaks of silver. Peavey didn't know her age, but assumed she was in her late forties, though she could be older. She obviously worked to keep herself slim and in shape.

He had never seen the woman wear anything other than sharp business attire, but tonight he was surprised to see her in snug designer blue jeans and a loose-fitting blouse that did little to hide her curves. The woman was shapely, to be sure, but no man, at least none that worked for her, would ever consider making a pass. Not if they valued their life.

"Andrew seems to think the situation has gotten out of hand, Anthony. From the mess up by the gate, I would tend to agree. Malik and I had to climb over it. And you know there are two dead bodies up there, right? Michael and David, I believe? Oh, and what the hell happened to my truck?"

"I don't know what all Andrew's told you, but I've got it under control." He flicked an angry glance at Aikman, who now stood in the doorway between the kitchen and the living room. The man was angling to come up a notch, take Peavey's position as something of a confidant and right hand to Meryl, Peavey could see it in the smug look Aikman wore. If he got the chance, he planned to smack that smug grin off his face.

"Do you? Have it under control? Really? Three dead men, a wrecked truck and no way in or out of here is what you consider "under control"? Some hero running around, trying to what, rescue our merchandise? A hero who is really just some loser nobody who's gotten the upper hand here? It doesn't sound like *anything* is under control, Anthony. It sounds to me like the whole damn thing is spiraling *out* of control."

Peavey heard the front door open and glanced toward the doorway Aikman was standing in, relieved to have a reason to look away from the woman's angry gaze.

The man who walked in stood around six-two, smooth-shaven head, dark brown skin with eyes to match. He seemed to glare at everything and everyone at all times. Peavey had met Malik years ago, when first joining Meryl. The thick scar running down the left side of the man's face was a testament to Meryl's anger.

Meryl turned, and Malik shook his head then took a position an arm's-length away from and behind the woman.

Peavey had never heard the big black man speak.

Nodding her head, Meryl indicated the kitchen table and said, "You look tense, Anthony, let's sit, talk, and figure out what you need to do to fix this."

The beads of sweat running down his back

made him itch, and now, having Malik behind him, out of sight, made his skin crawl. Meryl liked to handle things herself. She had no problem getting blood on her hands. That didn't mean she wouldn't have Malik do the work. The woman was volatile and unpredictable.

Peavey knew one of two things. He would walk away from this table. Or he wouldn't.

Chapter 37

Joe eased the door open a fraction of an inch at a time, keeping his eye close to the crack. He saw nothing, no one, but that didn't mean they weren't out there. The entire time he had been inside the barn they could have been posting an ambush, waiting, knowing all along where he was. Now, with the addition of two new figures, Joe understood that he couldn't just wait things out and hope for something to happen in his favor.

Once the door was open wide enough to allow him to slip through, he stopped and watched for another minute. Nothing moving other than the night breeze.

He kept low, in a crouch, and slipped out the door, closing it softly behind him. He left it open just a crack, so that the hasp wouldn't strike the staple and lock again, fearing even that tiny sound would be heard inside the house, as if they were possessed of not just evil intent, but supernatural hearing.

The only window that would afford someone in the house a direct view of the barn was on the wall facing him. The front of the house was angled away just enough to make viewing from those windows difficult. He hoped.

Moving swiftly while staying as silent as possible, Joe moved across the fifty yards of driveway and tall grass toward the window. At the house he knelt on the ground next to the window with his back pressed against the wall.

He could hear people talking, but he was unable to make out any words. They must be in another room, their voices muffled by the wall and distance. Joe pulled in a deep breath, dreading the idea of moving around the house, further away from the barn and the woods. He didn't feel safe in either, but out here in the open, it seemed like he was offering himself up for slaughter.

He moved toward the rear corner and peeked around. To Joe it felt as if he had spent more time simply watching the area for kidnappers than anything else. No movement, no shadowy shapes suddenly appearing from the darkness.

Joe moved around the corner in a crouch, eyes focused on the area of light spilling from one of the two windows on this end of the house. He reached the first window easily, and crouched next to it, listening. The voices were slightly louder now, but he was still unable to make out distinct words.

Just as Joe ducked lower to move past the window, a shadow fell on the ground in the circle of light coming through the glass. He pressed himself against the side of the house and held his breath like the man inside could hear even the faintest exhalation. The irrational fear that his hammering heart could be heard like a fist pounding on the weathered old siding filled him with dread and he leaned forward and inch, just so his back wasn't up against the house.

The huge shadow stayed where it was for several minutes. Joe imagined the size wasn't a distortion created by the light, but that the person behind the window really was a giant, one that was about to smash a massive hand through the glass, reach out and drag him inside to grind his bones to powder.

Unable to hold his breath any longer, Joe released it softly and began taking long, slow breaths through his nose. The interminably long wait, which might have lasted no more than two minutes ended when the shadow shifted and disappeared.

Joe moved, dropping low and crawling under the window. He felt exposed, with his back to the light. Once he reached the other side he crouched against the house once more and moved to the next window. Just past that was the back door. Light came through the window, but Joe was relieved that the bulb above the door was dark. Less light was better.

Pressing up against the house, his head close to the side of the window, Joe listened. He could hear the voices clearly, though they were still muffled. He focused on what they were saying and could just make out the words. He wasn't about to move closer.

The woman's voice was saying *"So he's just some random person, who happened to see Mike and Dave grab the girl and went into hero mode and jumped on the van?"*

"Exactly. It's all just some freak chance. He's lucky, nothing more." Joe recognized

Peavey's voice. It was a voice he would probably hear in his nightmares for the rest of his life, that is, if his life lasted past tonight.

Even muffled and distant, the anger in the woman's voice came through to Joe loud and clear. *"If those two weren't dead, they would be, Anthony."*

Anthony? Was that Peavey's first name? It seemed so mundane, Anthony. He wondered if people ever called him Tony. His mother, maybe, but Joe seriously doubted that anyone else did.

"I agree. I'd hoped to handle this without involving you. I'll get it taken care of, Meryl, I guarantee it."

Joe was surprised to detect a tone of nervousness in Peavey's voice.

"You're damn right you're going to handle, Anthony. I want this nobody dead before sunrise, understand?"

Of course you do, Joe thought. He couldn't make out Peavey's quiet response.

"Between you and Andrew, you've got three special orders here, correct?"

Another voice, one Joe didn't recognize, said, *"Yes, that' right."* Possibly Andrew, which would make him the owner of the restored Camaro.

"Malik and I are going to take them with us. Senator Wilkins is pitching his usual bitch, but he's also offering an extra ten thousand for an early delivery. As for the other two, I don't want to risk losing them should you screw this up. The

rest you'll hand off in two days like you're supposed to."

Joe rested his head against the house and balled his hands into tight fists. They were going to take three of the girls out. A U. S. senator was paying for one of them, offering extra money to get her early. It was too much to process and Joe knew that he couldn't stop them from taking the girls. Outnumbered, outgunned, and woefully unprepared, the only thing he could do was let them go.

A sense of failure washed over Joe, pounding him in a wave of grief and anger. This shouldn't be happening. It shouldn't be possible, not here, not in America. Joe was unable to fathom the idea that this Meryl, this woman, would sell young girls. How could she? Just... how?

"I want this Joe Pruitt dead, Anthony. Leave his body in four different states. I'm sure you've got something around here you can use for that. And get that truck and body off the front gate. What if some idiot were to turn in here and see that. You'd have state and county here in a heartbeat."

Joe leaned forward getting ready to move. He had to get back to the barn, think of something. He needed a plan.

Joe heard Meryl say, *"Have two of your men get the girls ready and help us take them to the gate. Malik, take one more walk around the house before we go."*

"One of my guys can walk the house,"

Peavey said.

"You don't have any more guys, Anthony. Malik will do it. I can trust him not to screw up."

Joe's anger was replaced with terror. Malik was going to take a walk around the house and there was no way he could make it to the barn without being seen. He cast a frantic glance around the dark yard just as he heard the front door open.

Forgetting caution, Joe jumped up and took off at a run, angling for the woods, praying he could cross the seventy-five yards to the tree-line before Malik came around the side of the house.

Chapter 38

Every raw nerve was firing on high as Joe ran towards the trees. Each wound protested the exertion with jolts of pain. He didn't slow down or bother to look back until he hit the edge of the trees and leapt over a rotted stump in the middle of thick overgrowth. If Malik or one of the others saw him, he would know by either the shout or the bullet he got in the back.

He sprawled out flat, turned over, and poked his head above the stump just far enough to see a blurry image of the yard and house. Just as he was raising his eye above the level of the top of the stump, he saw a shadow that could only be Meryl's gunman, Malik rounding the corner of the house.

Joe was unable to make out anything other than the man's movement. A minute after he appeared, the big shadow walked past the lighted rear window Joe had been crouching next to less than two minutes ago, listening.

Too close, he thought. Too damn close. He felt he should be getting used to it by now. The night had been full of close calls.

As soon as the man moved around the far corner of the house and out of sight, Joe popped up from his hiding place and used the stump to get back over the thick brush and crackling leaves without making noise. Back in the grass, Joe ran for the barn, hoping to get at least behind it, into that forgotten spot at the corner of the woods.

Together, fear, exhaustion and rage all worked to distort time. It seemed to Joe that his mad sprint might have taken far longer than it actually had, a nightmare marathon that would never end. Minutes could be misshapen to feel like hours, or they were twisted into appearing like only a nanosecond had passed.

The run from his hiding spot behind the stump to the nearest edge of the barn took less than a minute, and he stayed right at the very edge of the trees, using their deep darkness to mask his movement.

Just as Joe came close to the barn, the front door opened, and people paraded out. Joe nearly dived the last few feet. His heart tripping over itself between the exercise and fear. He was certain that it would simply give up and stop any time now, tired of being overworked.

With the barn between him and those exiting the house, Joe moved to the far corner, crouched as low as possible in the dark, forgotten corner of tall grass, and watched the people, no more than indistinct, dark shapes, against the black backdrop of the trees on their opposite side.

He counted six, with the three shortest shadows in the middle. Joe had no way of knowing who they were, or how many had been chosen to go with them to get the girls over the gate. Would they have left the house empty, the remaining girls unguarded? Not likely, even if they weren't concerned about a marauding nobody do-gooder like himself running around out here in the dark.

Joe felt the anger at the three girls being taken creep up again, now that he wasn't worried about being spotted. If he were to charge out there in an attempt to prevent them being removed from the property and from eventual rescue, he would only hasten his own death. Nothing would be gained from it, yet he still felt that he had let them down somehow. That it was his fault they were being marched out into the night to end up as the property of some pervert to whom money and power meant more than basic human decency. Joe's frustration was palpable, almost a living thing.

Once they were gone, they were gone, and there was nothing he could do.

Joe recalled something he had heard Meryl mention that only added to his impotent rage. *Senator Wilkins is pitching his usual bitch, but he's also offering an extra ten thousand for an early delivery.*

Senator Wilkins? Joe followed politics about as closely as the next guy, which meant not much. The woman had to have been referring to Dorian Wilkins. Joe knew the man was a Democrat, but he couldn't remember what state the senator represented. He was known for his loud, obnoxious rants directed at both his political adversaries as well as members of his own party.

To Joe, "pitching his usual bitch" sounded like the Senator had regular dealings with these people.

He knew, now, there were more levels and layers to this than he could possibly imagine. Even if he were to somehow save the girls inside the house, this would still be happening. Girls would go missing. Families would still lose loved ones. Mothers, daughters, sisters, friends; so many vulnerable women and girls out there, someone would take advantage of them, or would simply snatch them from the street just like he had seen.

Joe pulled his rage tight around him like a cloak. He wished he could stop them all, end the suffering and the hurt of so many people. He accepted that it wasn't possible, but he was determined to at least save the ones inside that house.

The shadow-people walking through the night disappeared, passing behind the screen of trees that blocked the upper part of the drive.

As much as it pained him to consider, those girls were now out of his reach. There was nothing he could do for them. But the ones left in the house, those he could help.

Joe waited until he saw a single shadow return several minutes later. Whoever it was had stood at the front door for a while, surveying the dark yard and the woods beyond. Yeah, keep looking, asshole, Joe thought.

The man finally went back inside, and the moment the door closed, Joe crouch-walked to the barn door and pulled it open just enough to slip inside.

Once the door was closed behind him, he

walked to the rear van with his hands out, blind in the darkness. He retrieved the charging phone and checked it. The battery was up to 87%. Good enough.

Chapter 39

Joe couldn't rely on his minimal skill with the handgun. He knew that by the time he had aimed and taken a shot, the others would most likely have riddled him with a full magazine's worth of ammunition or more.

Using the light on the cell phone Joe walked the barn once more, examining everything. There were farm tools, and some were sharp or heavy. He had to even out the odds. They saw him as lucky, and maybe he was, but he thought he might be able to use that. Joe couldn't say for sure what Peavey and the others expected, but he was sure they wouldn't expect Joe to bring the fight to them in any way.

After selecting several items, he walked back to the rear-most van, the one he had been in earlier in the day and lay the implements across the driver's seat. He examined the double-bladed axe, the spading fork, and the hammer. Each of them would require him to get close, within arms reach or closer, to be of any real use.

It was all he had. But now, how to use them? Joe turned and leaned against the van, pinching the bridge of his nose, and swiping the fingers up past the corners of his eyes, tracing his eyebrows. His hand spread out, and he wiped his palm up his forehead, then all the way back down his face, his fingers rasping over the days growth of stubble on his cheeks. He paused, gripping his chin with one hand, thinking.

He had left the van door open, and the glow of the interior light reflected back to him from the rear taillights and chrome of the classic car. That car was Andrew A. Aikman's pride and joy.

Joe released his chin and stood a little straighter, an idea coming to him. While he thought it might have some success, he wished he knew how many men Peavey had inside the house, and would they all come out after him?

Probably not. No way would Peavey leave the girls unguarded.

With the sprouting seeds of an idea growing in his mind, Joe began to pace off the barn. There was very little space between the wall and the vans on the right side, just enough room for a man to turn sideways and squeeze through for nearly the entire length of the building. The vans were also bumper to bumper, with less than an inch of space between them. The nose of the front van was less than a foot away from the back wall.

There was enough room between the front van and the car for Joe to open either door without hitting the other vehicle. The space behind the car was approximately ten feet of open dirt to the barn door.

Standing behind the rear van, closest to the door, Joe held the axe and made a practice half-swing. There wasn't enough space to swing wide. What if I come up from underneath, connect with the guy's crotch? He thought.

Joe stopped, standing there with a double-bladed axe in his hands, realizing that he was actively planning the violent murder of another human being. The part of himself he had always seen as the Average Joe type, work hard, pay the bills, try to have a little fun in life, be decent to others, felt a sense of anger and disgust at what he was considering. Joe Pruitt didn't want to kill anyone. But these men wanted to kill him, and they wouldn't have the same qualms about it that he did.

Joe could also see the near-absurdity of what he was thinking. He was planning to thin the numbers, even things up in his favor. Using gardening tools.

He felt he had no options left. He was unable to trust any local authorities enough to make a phone call, which left only him.

"These odds suck," Joe muttered softly to the dark barn.

He took several more minutes, considering his plan and mentally psyching himself up for what he was about to do. If Peavey and the others wanted to kill him, he was damn sure going to make them work for it.

Joe retrieved his makeshift weapons and closed the van door, plunging the barn back to pitch black. With the light from the phone, Joe got everything as ready as he possibly could. He placed his hand on the half of the door he had initially come through, let the phone go dark, then pushed it open several inches. The gap was obvious.

Once more, Joe keyed the screen on, went to recent call history and tapped the last number called.

Chapter 40

"You think we can use one of the vans to pull the truck off the gate and get Mike's body out? Put both his and Dave's bodies in the back, and pull it up far enough to be out of direct sight of anyone that might pull up to the gate?"

Peavey nodded to Aikman. "That might work. One of the vans has a tow-strap. You think there's any chain or tow-rope in the barn?"

"There might be, we can look," Aikman replied.

Peavey glanced at the man with the scale tattoos covering half his face when he said, "No keys for the truck. We'd have to drag it. Can't steer, and Porter said the tires were all flat."

Peavey sighed. "We'll just have to make it work. We've got to get it done well before first light though. People out here in bum-fucked-nowhere get started early."

"We need to get this guy to come in. I want this over. Aikman, get on my computer and see if you can find out where his wife and daughter are."

Peavey ignored the icy look Aikman shot him before moving to the kitchen table.

Peavey walked to the refrigerator and opened the door. He reached for a bottle of water and paused when his phone buzzed and chimed in his pocket. Probably Meryl with more instructions, he thought and let the fridge close.

Looking at the phone, he was surprised to

see it was Glenn's phone again. "He's calling."

"Who is?" Aikman asked.

"Joe, damn it, who else."

Peavey tapped the screen, accepting the call. With the phone pressed to his ear he said, "Yes, Joe?"

"Hey, Peavey, put me on speaker, I want all your people to hear me."

"Why would I do that, Joe? And what makes you think you're in a position to make demands?"

"Just do it, damn it. I'm tired of all this crap. I want it over."

Peavey shrugged to himself. Maybe he could use whatever Joe was doing to get the man to come in. Why not?

"Fine Joe, but just because I want this over as well."

Peavey pulled the phone away from his face and tapped the screen. "Okay Joe, you're on speaker."

Peavey shrugged at Aikman, who was now looking a question at him. The man's face said, Why, what point is there?

"Can all of your people hear me? I want to hear them say they can hear me."

"No, Joe. Serves no purpose."

"It serves my *purpose, Peavey. Damn it. Please. I want to know they can all hear what I have to say."*

Porter, Nate and Scales had all drifted into the room. Peavey looked around at each and back at the phone held out in his hand. The weary desperation in Joe's voice brought a smile to his face. Fine, let the man have what he wanted. "Ok, Joe. Let's just consider it the last request of a dead man walking."

"Call it whatever you want, Peavey. I don't care anymore."

Peavey nodded to the other men, and each in turn said, "Yeah, I can hear you," including Aikman.

"Satisfied, Mr. Average Joe? We can all hear your dying wish."

"Yeah, you're real fucking clever, Peavey. I may not be some trained badass, but I've still gotten three of your people, haven't I?"

Peavey could hear the instant change in Joe's voice. From weak, tired and begging to hard and icy. He didn't like it.

"I just wanted to make sure that each of your people know that I'm gonna try real damn hard to kill every one of you. I'm done playing around out here, Peavey. I was fighting back, earlier. Just trying to stay alive, you know? Now, well, things are different."

Peavey's voice shaped to a dark edge, "Joe, you're a dead man, you know that. You end this shit now and I'll lose your daughter's address. Keep playing games…"

"Screw you, Peavey," Joe interrupted.

Peavey ground his teeth together and spat, "I'm not gonna let these guys kill you, Joe. I'm gonna make sure they bring you to me. Then I'm gonna have some fun with you. You'll beg me to kill you long before I get done."

"I'm pissed those girls were taken out of here. Who was the woman, Peavey?"

Peavey's brow bunched up as he thought. Joe was close enough to watch the house. He had seen Meryl take the girls out. Where was he watching from?

"Trust me, Joe, she's someone you don't ever want to meet."

"Yeah, maybe." Joe fell silent for a moment and Peavey was about to speak when the man said, *"Hey, Peavey, which one of your people is Andrew A. Aikman?"*

Aikman shot up from the chair, his face a knot of confusion and anger. "How the hell do you know my name?!"

"Did I pronounce that right? Like the Cowboy's quarterback?"

"Listen, asshole!"

"No, you listen, asshole!"

Peavey was surprised at the vehemence coming from the phone. Joe Pruitt no longer sounded like a whipped and worn out man ready to give up and die. He sounded like someone ready for blood.

"I just wanted you to know, Andrew, that I'm sorry about your car. It really was a gorgeous Camaro. I've always wanted one just like it, except in blue, not this shitty green color."

Peavey shouted, "He's in the fucking barn!" at the same time Aikman yelled "You mess with my car, I'll kill you!"

Peavey's hand shot out, grabbing Aikman's

shoulder just as the man turned to bolt for the door. "He's trying to bait you, damn it!"

Aikman tried to shrug Peavey's grip, his face burning crimson, rage flaring in his eyes like sparks. "My car!"

All three of the other men moved toward the back door. Peavey said, "No, Porter you stay here. Nate, Scales, get to the barn and bring me that son-of-a-bitch!"

The man with the tattooed face canted his head and squinted, glaring at Peavey, "Scales? "My name is…"

"I DONT GIVE A FUCK WHAT YOUR GOD DAMN NAME IS! GO GET HIM!" Peavey felt himself on the verge of losing his last shred of patience, and possibly sanity.

"You're dead, asshole! I'll kill you myself!"

"You guys have been trying that all night long, Andrew A. Aikman. Try harder."

The phone went silent just as Nate and Scales charged out the back door.

Chapter 41

Joe ended the call and powered the phone down completely, not wanting to take a chance that it might somehow give him away at the worst possible moment. Murphy's Law and all that.

Joe stood inside the barn with his back to the right half of the double doors, less than an arm's length from the edge. He watched the shadow of the gap he had left there and waited, knowing someone would be coming, and fast. He had to time it just right.

What could have been an hour or fifteen seconds later, a man yanked the door open and stepped into the barn. The moonlight wasn't quite as bright as earlier, but it created a patch of light just inside the doors and the kidnapper stood in the center of it. Joe whispered, "Hey," and the man turned toward him.

Between the van and the door, there wasn't enough room to swing the axe wide and aim for the man's head. Instead, Joe gripped it like a golf club, and swung up like he was trying to smash a golf ball out into the stratosphere.

Joe had misjudged the distance as well as the speed of the man's reaction. The man took a half-step back as he turned toward Joe, his hand coming up to aim a pistol into the dark. That half-step back prevented the axe from connecting solidly with the man's crotch.

The gun fired a single shot, high and to Joe's

right, punching a hole in the wall a foot below the ceiling.

The axe caught the front of the man's shirt and split it from the abdomen all the way to the breastbone. The fabric spread apart followed a second later by the man's skin opening wide.

Joe stared as the man sunk to his knees, a strange "Uh-uh-uh" falling from the kidnapper's gaping mouth as they both watched what was inside him begin to spill out, folding over his hands in shimmery loops and whorls and dropping to the ground with a solid, wet plop.

Jesus, I... I unzipped him, Joe thought.

Joe could see nothing but reflected moonlight when the dying man turned his eyes up to him. It was a small relief. He had already watched the light of life fade from another man's eyes tonight, and it wasn't something he wanted to make a habit of.

Joe was jerked from shocked revulsion at the sound of a voice from outside.

"Nate, did you hit him? Nate?

Nate's head turned toward the toward door, and his mouth opened but the only thing that came out in response to the caller was "ah-huh-huh" and he toppled forward, onto the steaming pile of his own intestines.

Joe let the axe fall, and he dropped to the ground, backing away from the edge of the door just enough to stay in shadow. He tugged the hammer in his belt free, and on all fours, out of the line of sight, he waited for the next man to come through the door.

He saw the man's gun, first, held out in front, then his face, covered in geometric tattoos. Fish scales? A muttered "Holy shit! Nate?"

The kidnapper stepped through the door, toward his fallen companion. Unlike the axe, Joe was able to swing the hammer in a wide arc. He was surprised when his aim was perfect, and the flat face of the hammer connected with the man's kneecap. Joe felt the patella explode under the impact.

The tattooed man screamed, dropped his pistol and fell to his knees. He cried out again when his smashed knee hit the ground and he toppled over sideways, next to the body of his dying friend.

Joe spun the hammer in his hand so that the nail-pulling claws were now facing down, lunged forward, and brought the hammer down hard on the man's temple.

Bone cracked, and the claws gouged two furrows of skin from the man's head.

Joe drew the hammer back. The kidnapper threw up a hand to block the next blow and Joe batted it away. Teeth clamped together, a growl of rage pushing between his lips, Joe brought the hammer down again with all the strength in his shoulder and arm.

The claws punched through with ease, bone shattered, blood splattered Joe's hammer hand and his face. The kidnapper's left eye popped free of it's socket from the pressure cause by the blow, hanging by its optic nerve across the bridge of his nose.

A few twitches and the man went still.

Joe tried to pull the hammer free, but it was lodged firmly in the skull. Wet noises and the sound of cracking bone brought a wave of nausea and Joe felt his gorge rise. He left the hammer buried where it was, sticking up from the man's head at an odd angle. He wouldn't need it now.

Two men. He had counted five on the phone call. That would leave Peavey, Aikman, and one other in the house. Unless they had duped him and not everyone had spoken.

It didn't matter. Joe knew that he could wait no longer to take the fight to them. He stood there, over the dead bodies. Bodies of men he had just killed. The sight, the smell, all of it made Joe feel sick. Underneath his anger and disgust at having been forced to kill. Under the stomach-turning nausea at the brutality of his own actions, Joe felt justified. They were kidnappers, selling little girls. They wanted him dead and would have gladly murdered him.

Still deeper, he felt that sense of grim satisfaction. They deserved to die. He was no vigilante, it wasn't his place to exact retribution for their crimes. But he had. He had done exactly that. Exacted retribution of the most vicious kind.

Joe turned away from the bodies and bent to retrieve the axe. Standing there, the axe resting on his shoulder, he listened. No footsteps, no one calling out to the men on the ground. Joe didn't even hear night sounds. He imagined for a moment that he had gone deaf, maybe from the gunshot so close to his head. Then, he registered the sound of his own breathing.

The night seemed to be holding its own breath, pensive, waiting for the next act of violence, the next cry of pain.

Joe stepped into the small circle of moonlight falling between the open doors, kicking away the foot of the tattooed man. He stood there watching the house to see if anyone else would come.

Joe Pruitt stepped from the barn, one hand on the pistol in his jacket pocket, the other holding the axe up on his shoulder, and walked toward the house. He would make a circuit of the entire place, look for a weak spot, an opportunity.

He was no longer the one running. He wasn't hiding, waiting to die. They were. They just didn't know it.

Behind him, from the barn, he heard music, a short clip of a popular hard rock tune, repeated several times. When that fell silent, it was followed by the stock ringtone of another cell phone.

A faint, dark grin creased his mouth. Keep calling, he thought, they won't be answering.

Chapter 42

"Neither one is answering," Porter said, looking hard at Peavey.

"Damn it! This is bullshit!"

"I'm going to check on my car, Peavey."

"The hell you are, Andrew. That's just what this asshole wants. He might have ambushed the other two and is hoping for another one to come along."

"Screw you. You've lost control of this whole thing. It's your fault this son of a bitch is even here! Porter, let's go look."

Porter slipped his phone back into his pocket and walked toward Aikman. Peavey's hand shot out and grabbed Porter by the shoulder. "You aren't going anywhere unless I tell you to," he growled at the big man.

Porter slapped Peavey's hand away and stepped in close, almost nose to nose. "Touch me again, and you'll eat your own hand."

Aikman glared at Peavey. "You've lost control, Peavey. I'm handling this now. Meryl wants this guy dead and I'm going to take her his head. You stay here and watch the girls. A few of them are probably waking up, ready for a fresh dose."

Peavey glared right back at Aikman. The last bit of control he had was slipping away, and he knew it, but if he could finish Joe and end this, be the one to bring Meryl his head, then he might be able to salvage the situation. "Fine, do whatever you want. I hope he pops both of you in the fucking head." Peavey turned and stalked off toward the holding room, his face bright red.

He heard the front door open and close a minute later and went back to the kitchen, buttoning up his shirt. He tugged the pistol in his belt free and laid it on the table next to the computer. Sitting down in front of the lap-top, Peavey brought up the most recent information that Aikman had found on Joe's family. He needed leverage.

A minute after Porter and Aikman left the house he heard wild shouts coming from the direction of the barn. He could just barely make out the string of expletives and threats of violence directed at Joe.

Peavey chuckled at Aikman's rage.

Chapter 43

Joe had just rounded the back corner of the house when he heard the front door open. He stopped and pressed himself against the side of the house, staying out of sight, watching. Two dark shapes, one taller than the other, came into view, heading straight for the barn. The shorter man was out in front and moving faster than the taller man. Joe waited.

A light popped on in the barn followed a second later by a yell, then shouts of rage and promises of violence. Joe grinned. The shorter man must have been Aikman, and he had found the spading fork Joe had shoved through the rear window of the Camaro just seconds before he had made his call only a short while ago.

"You're dead! I'm going to kill you slow, Joe! I'm gonna shove this thing though your FAAAACE!"

Joe's smiled widened. There had been little in the past few hours to take any real pleasure in, but the unhinged screaming coming from the barn was worth enjoying.

The larger of the two men stepped back outside the now-wide open barn door and looked around.

"Do you see him? Porter! Do you see him!?"

The big man turned around and said, *"I don't see anything. He can't be far, though."*

Joe ducked behind the corner, thinking. If

Aikman and this Porter were out at the barn, and they hadn't tried to fool him on the phone call, that meant that Peavey was alone in the house with the girls.

Joe turned and stalked toward the back door, passing the windows he had hidden below earlier, when listening to Meryl. He didn't hide this time.

At the back door, Joe's hand hesitated at the door knob for two heartbeats as he considered what he was about to do. He heard a voice talking, just beyond the door, and lowered his hand. Had there been more people in the house?

"Yes, ma'am, were afraid that your ex-husband has had an emotional breakdown. He's become violent. We wanted to let you know, and possibly ask for your help. Maybe if you were to talk to him, you could get him to come in before he hurts himself, or anyone else."

Joe's head cocked to the side, like a dog listening to a radio, his face quizzical. Ex-husband? Emotional breakdown? Talk to him? What the hell? Then it hit Joe just who Peavey was talking to.

He threw open the door and took two steps inside the house. Peavey was seated at a kitchen table, in front of a lap-top computer, with a phone up to his ear. His back was to the door, and to Joe.

Peavey held up a finger, as if asking Joe to wait, then he placed a hand over the phone and turned as he asked, "What happened, Andrew? Did he do…"

187

Peavey's eyes opened wide and he jumped up from the chair when he saw the man standing there with a double-bladed axe over his shoulder.

Joe's eyes seemed to flash with rage as he shouted, "Anne! Hang up the phone, he's a killer! Hang up the phone, Annie!"

A tiny voice came from Peavey's phone, almost unintelligible. *"Joe? What's going on? Joe? Are you..."*

Joe took a step toward Peavey.

Peavey lunged for the pistol on the table, brought it up and fired a shot that went wide in his haste.

In one swift move Joe dropped the axe from his shoulder, took it in both hands and swung for the man's neck.

Peavey tried to jump back, away from the wicked edge coming at him and fell backward over the chair he had just been sitting in. The gun roared again, the bullet firing up into the ceiling. His phone flew from his hand, shattering the screen as it hit the floor. Peavey's head connected with the edge of the countertop behind him and he went down, crumpling like a cloth doll.

The weight of the axe and the force of Joe's swing carried the tool around and the head slammed into the wall next to him, biting deep. Joe tried to yank it free, but the blade must have found and buried itself into a stud, because it wouldn't come loose easily.

All he wanted, at that moment, was to rip the axe from the wall and bury it deep in

Peavey's head. He left the axe sticking out from the wall, reached into his pocket and grabbed the pistol.

Joe raised the gun in one hand and took aim at Peavey's head. Between the flood of adrenaline pumping through his blood and the hammering of his heart, Joe was unable to keep the barrel from wavering from side to side. He gripped the pistol in both hands, took a deep breath, then another, consciously willing his heartrate to slow down.

Joe's finger rested tightly in the trigger as his mind processed the idea that he was about to shoot and kill and unconscious man. He kidnaps and sells little girls to the highest bidder, Joe reminded himself.

Joe caught a blur out of the corner of his eye and turned to see what might have been a massive truck barreling down on him. He tried to swing the gun around, but it was far too late. He jerked the trigger, as if simply firing the gun would magically stop his attacker.

Porter hit Joe high, knocking him to the floor. The gun flew from Joe's hand and he reached out, grabbing a handful of Porter's shirt and pulling the big man down with him. Both crashed into the kitchen table, sending it across the floor. Chairs flipped and scattered, and Joe hit the side edge of one with his back.

The pain was unreal, and he was positive that his back was broken. A broken back meant he was a dead man. Fighting back, not just against Porter, but also against the idea that he was going to die here and now, Joe pounded a fist into the side of Porter's head. Pain flared through his knuckles and the man's head rocked to the side.

Porter replied in kind. The massive fist, it looked to Joe like a Volkswagen coming right at his face, slammed into his jaw and rocked his head back, rapping it on the hard floor. He heard the crack of bone, felt white-hot pain through his entire face. He felt his jaw dislocate from the blow. A second one, on the other side of his face, shoved the jaw back to its original position.

Joe tried not to scream. The sound came out more like a sob.

The massive man above him drew back for another swing, and Joe knew for sure that if it connected, he was out. Like a light. Darkness. Dead.

He rocked a knee upward as hard as he was able with limited room. He was rewarded when Porter let out a pained "OOF!". Joe threw himself sideways, twisting underneath the larger man, bucking and tossing. He pushed up, getting his knees under him, and his hands, then he threw an elbow backward, catching Porter in the mouth. He scrambled forward, out from under the big man, and crawled two feet. He spun around, to see Porter.

Both men stood up at the same time. Joe was shakier, his feet seeming to be planted on the deck of a storm-tossed ship.

Blood flowed freely from Porter's mouth, which made the big grin he was giving Joe even creepier, as if he were enjoying this.

Behind Porter, Joe caught a glimpse of another man coming through the door. Aikman. He was holding a pistol at his side.

Porter spat out a wad of blood, a Rorschach image of violence on the old tile floor and said, "Tougher than I thought you'd be."

Joe wanted to respond but his jaw hurt so much, that speaking right then felt like more of a chore than it was worth.

Joe backpedaled as Porter lurched forward, but he was still feeling stunned from the blows to the head, and the huge kidnapper moved far faster than Joe thought should be possible. In the next instant, Porter had his arms around Joe in a violent embrace, squeezing, pulling him in tight.

It felt to Joe like his ribcage was being compressed, squashing his heart and lungs. He was unable to draw a full breath, and the dizziness from the punches to the head were only compounded by black spots forming at the edges of his vision.

Acting out of survival alone, with no thought, Joe balled his fists up as tight as he could with his thumbs sticking out to the side. He swung them up with everything he had left, which wasn't much.

It was enough.

His thumbs drilled hard into Porter's ears.

Porter let out a scream that was more female than Joe would have expected. His hands flew up to the sides of his head, and Joe dropped to the ground, crumpling at Porter's feet.

He forced himself to keep moving. Aikman was still there, just watching as he and Porter battled. Joe scooted backward on the floor and stood. He could see the axe handle sticking out sideways from the wall behind Porter, meaning the axe head was behind him, protruding from the wall.

Without hesitation, Joe charged, screaming wordlessly, just raw noise and rage. He hit Porter just below the sternum and shoved backward, driving with his legs. Porter pawed at him, pulled at his shirt, slammed a fist into his back just once before another "OOF!" popped from his mouth. His hands flopped to his sides, hanging, his hands making smaller and smaller circles as they swung. Joe looked up at Porter's face, his eyes were wide and tracking back and forth, looking to Aikman, then back at Joe. His mouth moved, oddly fish-like, but no sound came out.

Joe was surprised to see a tear track down the huge killer's face.

He didn't have time to ponder what was going through Porter's mind right then. In the sudden stillness of the room, Joe heard a click from his left and felt a cold spot against the side of his head.

Chapter 44

"Don't move, asshole," Aikman grumbled.

Pumped on both adrenaline and pain, Joe ignored the command and turned to face the other man. The gun traced a chill line across his face. When he stopped, the barrel was pressed against the bridge of his nose right between his eyes.

This pistol was familiar to Joe, he couldn't remember the make or model, but he was certain it was a 9mm. At point blank range, it would carve a nice hole all the way through his head.

Looking directly into Aikman's eyes, he said, "What is it they say in the old-west movies? You've got me dead-to-rights? Pull the trigger, Andrew A. Aikman, Camaro owner and kidnapping asshole." Joe understood, somewhere in the back of his mind, that he should be utterly terrified right then. He should be begging for his life, pleading to stay alive even another minute.

Instead, he was goading the man holding a gun to his face.

Aikman grinned, and Joe could see the smug satisfaction on the man's face. But there was still work to be done, and playing tough-guy games with Aikman wasn't one of them. He lunged to the left, and struck out with his right hand, shoving Aikman to the side.

Aikman jerked the trigger, and Joe winced at the roar of the gun so close to his head. He felt the heat of the blast and the passage of the bullet.

Thankfully, that was all he felt.

Joe pushed with his left foot and darted back toward Aikman, jamming himself in close, preventing another shot. He grabbed the man's wrist, forcing the gun up and away and wrapped his other arm around Aikman's head and neck, pulling him close.

Andrew landed a punch to Joe's right side, hitting the flesh wound from Evan's gun earlier in the night. Joe grunted at the impact and sudden burst of pain, reacting by ramming a knee up and aiming for the man's crotch as he had done to Porter. Aikman twisted, and Joe caught his thigh instead.

Andrew pulled the trigger several more times, the gun popping round after round into the ceiling. Bits of plaster broke way, and the room began to fill with white dust, as if they were fighting inside a thin cloud of talcum powder.

Joe shoved, trying to move the man backward, and Aikman resisted. They were locked in a stalemate of simply holding their ground. Punches and jabs were ineffectual.

Aikman glared at Joe and growled into his face, "My car, you son of a bitch."

Joe grinned back and through clenched teeth muttered, "You didn't see what I did to the engine."

Andrew's eyes widened, and he let loose with a roar. The pistol cracked again. The two men continued to dance around the room for a minute, locked in their absurd waltz of violence.

Joe, beginning to feel the pain in his side

and shoulder, knew he was getting tired, weaker. He had to stop this, put Aikman down. With few options left to him, Joe pulled the man close while he snapped his head forward, his forehead meeting the bridge of Aikman's nose with a clean, audible snap.

Andrew cried out, and the hand he was punching Joe with flew up to his nose, blood surging through his fingers, cascading down his face. Joe drew back and launched a punch straight for Aikman's face, smashing the man's fingers into his nose.

With Aikman off balance and hurting, Joe shoved with his shoulder, drove the man back against the wall and pummeled his face several more times with his right hand, still holding the gun up and pointing to the ceiling.

Aikman's head bounced off the wall, and his effort to push back was weak. Joe brought the hand holding the gun down while driving up with his right fist, smashing Aikman's elbow. The joint hyper-extended and Aikman cried out once more. This time with more of a wailing sob than anything else.

The gun dropped to the ground and Joe kicked at Aikman's feet. The man, unbalanced, slammed back against the wall again and slid down to sit on the floor with his legs out in front of him. His fight was gone. Blood bubbled out from his nose, covering the lower half of his face and drenching his shirt.

Joe leaned over with his hands on his knees, heaving air, trying to get a full breath in the cloud of dust swirling around the kitchen. On the floor, Aikman, blubbered and bubbled. Joe enjoyed seeing the tough-guy kidnapper in such a state.

After drawing several more deep breaths, Joe bent and picked up Aikman's pistol. He pointed it at the man, just looking down the sights, with the front post centered on the man's bleeding and swollen nose.

Aikman looked up at him and began to shake his head, slowly at first, then faster, back and forth. "No… no… no, please, don't… you don't have to…".

Joe lowered the barrel and pulled the trigger. The handgun roared once, the shock of the recoil travelling up his arm and into his shoulder. He grimaced at the pain and lowered the pistol.

Aikman grunted and look down, clamping his good left hand to the hole that had suddenly appeared in his lower abdomen. His broken right arm lay on the floor next to him like a thing detached. He sobbed, once, then again and passed out.

Joe didn't know if the man was dead, but part of him hoped not. He should die the slow, painful death of a gut shot, a final punishment before going straight to hell.

Joe turned to look at Peavey, still unconscious on the floor and caught Porter in the corner of his eye. Angling to look at the man, Joe was shocked to see his eyes still tracking Joe, leaking tears. A thick stream of bloody drool dripped from his chin to spatter on the floor at his feet.

Joe took several tentative steps toward the big man, then moved to the side, to see behind him. The blade of the axe head was buried deep in Porter's back, holding him up. It looked to Joe like the sharp steel had cleaved right through the man's spine, about six inches below the neck.

Joe took a step back, looked into Porter's eyes and whispered, "Damn." He then turned to Peavey and left the big man hanging there. He wouldn't waste a bullet on a mercy shot. Joe Pruitt had moved beyond any will toward mercy into a state of distilled hatred for these people and what they did.

Standing several steps away from Peavey, Joe raised the pistol again. His hand shook, the pain in his shoulder biting deep with each movement. He glanced at the shoulder and saw the wounds had reopened, that fresh blood was seeping through his makeshift bandage.

Something in Joe reminded him that he should care. Not about these men, but about himself and who he was. He should care that he had gut-shot a man, leaving him to die. He should care that he was refusing to give mercy of any kind to Porter. He should care that he was considering shooting an unconscious man.

He should take care not to leave every shred of himself and his own humanity here in this room, as dead as these men.

Peavey twitched and groaned, his head moved, as if he were waking.

Joe pulled the trigger. Two shots rang out,

hitting the man in the chest. The body jumped and shook with the impact. He would have kept firing, but the gun clicked on an empty chamber.

He dropped the empty pistol and turned away. With his back to Peavey and his eyes closed, Joe sobbed, once, hard. He felt it in his chest and lungs, in the massive knot forming in his throat. The single sob broke him open and he couldn't hold anything back.

He sank to his knees in the middle of the kitchen floor and wept. He had murdered. He had nearly been killed. Kidnapped little girls. Evil women that sold them. Pain, so much pain. All of it rushed out of Joe in great heaving sobs. Regret, sorrow, rage and loss; Joe felt it all.

Joe tilted his head back and released a wordless scream at the ceiling. It was the sound of hurt and sorrow and outrage. His balled fists pounded the floor until he felt pain in his knuckles. Holding them up, he could see where the skin had begun to split. His sobs and screams tapered off and he stared at his bloody knuckles, for a moment thinking about nothing, his mind going blank and still.

He finally glanced away from his hand, and at the room around him. Standing, Joe's eyes travelled quickly over the bodies of the three dead men, seeing them without really looking. He had seen more than enough blood for a lifetime in just the past few minutes.

He sucked in a deep breath, filling his lungs, releasing it when the ache in his ribs became uncomfortable. Porter may have cracked one or two, he thought.

Chapter 45

Peavey's shattered phone lay on the floor, it's cracked screen laying face up. Anne. Peavey had been talking to Anne. He picked up the phone and pressed the button to bring it to life. As shattered as it appeared, it still worked. It took several careful taps to get it to redial the last number called.

He held the phone up and listened.

"Hello?"

"Anne? Annie, listen, that call you got, it isn't what you might be thinking."

"Joe, what the hell is going on? What've have you done? Why are you calling from the policeman's phone number?"

"He wasn't a cop. I can't really explain any of it right now, Annie, I just didn't want you to worry."

"I'm more pissed than worried, Joe."

"I understand, Annie. I do. I'll explain it all when I can, I promise. Right now, I've got to go. There's some people that need my help." Joe's jaw ached fiercely, and every word hurt.

"Wait, Joe…"

"Bye, Annie. I'll talk to you soon. Tell Cady Lynn I love her."

Joe pulled the phone away from his face but couldn't get the end icon to work on the shattered screen. He flipped it over, popped the case and yanked the battery, dropping it all to the floor.

Walking through the kitchen, he angled for the hallway that led to the room where the girls were being held. Peavey and the others might be dead, but there was still work to be done.

After everything, he wasn't about to call the authorities and bring them here. He couldn't risk the responding officer being one that had been paid off by Peavey. Joe could just imagine the guy pulling up to the house, taking one look and just shooting him on the spot. Possibly calling someone, Meryl maybe, to come collect her merchandise. With an additional large cash payment for his services in dispatching Joe, of course.

Joe flicked on the light, and the few girls that were awake winced at the sudden brightness. There were six left bound to the small beds. Joe agonized over the three girls Meryl and Malik had taken with them. He could have rescued nine girls. He sighed and pushed the thought away. The ones in this room were the only thing that mattered just then.

"Girls, uh, my name is Joe, and I'm here to help you."

All six of the girls were coming awake now, and Joe kept talking as he went around the room, reassuring them, speaking softly. He had to go back to the kitchen and dig for the handcuff key, finding it in Aikman's pocket. Back in the room, he freed each girl, throwing a thin blanket over their shoulders, asking them to stay calm and be patient.

When Joe came to the girl he had first seen

snatched off the street he paused and reached out, as if to place a hand on her shoulder in comfort, or some sense of camaraderie, like they had somehow been in this together. In a sense they had, but she didn't know. He pulled his hand back when she flinched and pulled away. He gave her a weak and sad smile, for the moment, feeling uncomfortable with his own aching face.

When all the girls were unshackled, he backed away to the door and crouched there, leaning against the door-frame. He was beginning to feel the exhaustion setting in.

"Listen, um, girls. I think most of you know what happened. Some pretty bad people took you. I've, uh…" Joe thought about his words for a second. "I've taken them out, I guess."

One of the girls, slim, brown hair, green eyes surrounded by dark circles asked, "Can we – can we go home?" Her voice was weak and groggy.

"Soon, I hope. Were going to go to the FBI office. There's one in Little Rock, a little over an hour from here. I think that's what we need to do."

Another girl, blonde hair, slight and thin, Joe thought she couldn't be more than ten, asked, "Little Rock? Like, in Arkansas? I'm from Wisconsin. Where are we? How did I get here? I wanna go home. Please let me go home."

The girl's face crumpled into hard tears and Joe felt his own well up in his eyes. His heart broke for her, for each of them. He didn't know how to comfort the girl. He understood they were all terrified, and none had reason to trust him, but he hoped they would, just for a little while.

The other girls began to cry with her, each pleading to go home. Joe stood, every single joint and nerve protesting with jabs and pricks of pain. "Girls, I want to help you get home, and the best way for me to do that is to get you to an FBI office. I need you all to stay here, right here in this room and wait, please. There's a van in the barn, but the front gate is blocked. If you can hold on for ten or fifteen more minutes, please, I'll get you home. Okay?"

The girls were moving, clustering together, holding each other as Joe spoke, and now they all looked up at him, faces red and wet from crying, bubbles of snot forming at their noses as if they were just toddlers instead of teen and pre-teen girls.

Their silent stares seemed almost accusatory. He couldn't blame them. "I have a little girl, probably close to some of you in age. I just wanna get home to her, Okay? Give me a few minutes, please. And wait in here." Joe glanced back toward the kitchen, and said, "What's out there, it… it really… it isn't something you want to see."

A couple of the girls nodded, and Joe nodded back. "Okay. I'll be right back, and we can all get out of here."

He stalked back to the kitchen, pushing himself to keep moving despite how utterly exhausted he felt. He wanted coffee, but he would settle for some cold water, both to drink and to dump over his head.

Stopping at the refrigerator, Joe pulled open the door and was happy to find a nearly-full case of premium bottled water. There were several types of soda-pop as well. He grabbed six bottles of water, and a bottle of cola. He tucked several bottles of water under one arm, cracked the soda and tipped it back, drinking deeply. He hiccoughed and belched several times when the sweet, caffeinated, bubbly drink hit his stomach.

He took the bottles of water back to the girls, setting them on a bed. "Thought you gals might need some water. Wait here, I'll be back in a few minutes, then it should be ok for you all to, uh, leave the room."

Joe went back through the kitchen, turned into the living area that was surprisingly comfortable. It reminded him of his Great-Aunt Milly's house. Two short sofas sitting at a ninety-degree angle, a fireplace, two overstuffed chairs and a recliner. Warm, light-colored wood panel through most of the room. The widescreen TV seemed out of place, as if it were brought here later and just dropped into the middle of the room.

Through the front door, out into the night air, he paused again, turning back to the house. Something itched at the back of his mind, like he had missed something. He dismissed it as overreaction due to fatigue and began walking the driveway toward the front gate.

He took two more long swallows of the Coke, draining it, and dropped the bottle in the drive. He kept moving but it took him longer than he liked to get to the gate and the truck. Everything hurt, his face was swelling and he just wanted to sleep.

When he reached the truck, Joe found the keys in his pocket where he placed them earlier, slid into the cab, and started it up. Though the tires were all flat, the truck rolled forward easily enough, and Joe stopped about fifteen feet away from the gate, near Dave's body, which still lay in the middle of the drive.

Sliding back out, he walked to the gate and Mike's body, which lay crumpled on the ground in front of it, where it had fallen when he pulled the truck away. Blood had pooled out of the man's mouth, crusting over his chin and shirt. As distasteful as it was to Joe, he reached down, grabbed the dead man by the wrists and began to pull him to the side.

His shoulder felt like it was stuffed with shards of glass, and his face throbbed from the exertion. His back and sides hurt where Porter and Aikman had landed punches. Joe felt like one big walking doctor's diagram of pain. If he had to point to that sign they had in all ER rooms, the Wong-Baker pain scale, the one with the faces describing your pain, for those who were non-verbal, or couldn't accurately describe it, Joe would point to the end face, the one with the tears. Then he would draw a new face just past that one. A screaming face.

Mike's body was nearly stiff as a board, and his cold skin felt oddly rubber-like in Joe's hands. The gravel scraped and rolled noisily as Joe pulled him to the side, unceremoniously dropping him when he reached the far edge of the gate, out of the way of its swing.

Back at the gate itself, Joe wrapped both hands around the top bar and yanked. The gate was bent, jammed into place, and wouldn't open. He pulled at it several times, with no success.

He remembered that the gate had a magnetic release, but looking loosely, the way the gate was torqued, it had been pulled completely away from the latching mechanism. The gate should open.

"Damn it! Can't *something* be easy tonight?"

Joe leaned forward, on the gate, his arms extended, but the pain in his shoulder and ribs wouldn't let him take a moment in that position either. He stood, and turned back, looking at the truck. He walked back, opened the door and stared into the truck for a minute, thinking. Then he tilted the seat forward and reached behind it, within seconds he found what he was looking for. An emergency tow rope.

Joe returned the seat to its upright position, climbed in and started it up, leaving the door hanging open. The flat tires didn't want to grab the grass on the right side of the truck and it took longer than he wanted in getting the vehicle backed up to the gate. When he was two feet away, he stopped, left the truck running and climbed out. He looped the rope through the gate, in the middle of the latch-side post, hoping for the most leverage.

When it was tied as tightly as he could get it, Joe went back and tied the rope around and over the shin-crunching ball hitch sticking from the back. He sighed, tossed a silent prayer to the stars, climbed back in the truck, closed the door, and put the vehicle in drive.

Seconds later he was slammed backward in his seat. A metallic grinding crunch came from behind him, and the gate popped free. The truck lurched forward again, and Joe was slammed backward once more a second later when the gate reached the apex of it's swing and pulled at the hinges.

Joe pressed on the brake and shoved the gear-shift back to Park. He left the engine running and slipped back out. The gate was now wide open, more than enough to let the van through. The top hinge had torn away, leaving the gate hanging on the tow rope and the bottom hinge. Joe left it, went back and turned the truck off. Now he had to get the van, load these girls up, and get the hell out of there.

Chapter 46

Joe headed toward the barn as quickly as he could. It wasn't nearly as fast as he would have liked. He hobbled what he believed to be almost one-hundred and fifty yards from the gate to the barn on the gravel drive. He would have cut across the yard, and maybe even through the edge of the tree-line to get a straighter shot at the vehicles waiting in there, but it was dark, and if he were to find a chuck-hole and stumble, possibly breaking an ankle in the process, it would only make what he had to do even more difficult.

He passed the front door of the house and turned to watch it as he walked by, half expecting it to be thrown open by a mad Peavey or even a zombie-like Aikman. Guns blazing, raining a hail of bullets down on him.

He went by without incident and was half-way to the barn before he remembered that none of the keys had been in any of the vehicles when he had crawled around in them earlier during his search of the barn.

He stopped, sighed heavily, and turned back toward the house.

Minutes later he was back outside, having searched the pockets of all three dead men. From the time he had left the girls waiting, to now, it had only been about ten or fifteen minutes. It felt like hours.

He stood outside the front door, looking

back and forth toward the gate and the barn. There were two dead men at either place, and he had no idea who might have what keys. He loathed the idea of checking the men in the barn. Joe could see himself sifting through the pile of another man's insides searching for keys that might not be there.

He shuddered and turned toward the gate. Reason said that either Mike or Dave would have the keys for the rear van in the barn, as they had been the ones driving it when they brought the girls here with Peavey.

He trudged back toward the gate, the truck and the two dead men, forcing himself to move faster, hoping he would be able to stay upright for a few more hours at least. Might need to pound down another soda, he thought. The gravel rolled and scraped under his feet and he found himself almost mesmerized by the sound.

He shook his head, focused on moving forward, and got to Dave's body in minutes. He patted pockets, searched the man's jacket. Nothing.

He shuffled over to where he had left Mike's body. He went through the same procedure, patting pockets. He felt something hard inside Mike's right front jeans pocket and pushed two fingers down into the wet cloth. Joe knew it was soaked with the man's blood where he had been crushed between the truck and the gate.

His fingers found a point, then a jagged edge. He pinched and pulled, losing his grip once, then finally slipping the keys free. The electronic fob dangled from a ring with only the one key on it.

Joe wondered why none of the men had locked the vehicles. They had the ease of the electronic locks and the key-fob. Either they were lazy or forgetful, though he didn't really believe either. They had felt secure. Safe. They had never expected Joe Pruitt. He was glad they hadn't.

With keys in hand and his spirit buoyed somewhat by finding them, he made his way to the barn, his step a little faster and more surefooted, less shuffling and more walking.

Back at the barn, he tugged both doors wide. The light was still on, and he tried to only half-see the two gory bodies on the floor, their blood soaking into the dirt. The stench was awful. Joe would remember it for years. He was sure of it. The smell of feces, urine, blood and terror.

If he backed straight up he would narrowly miss both men.

Joe yanked the door open and slid into the van. The seat seemed to pull him in, and he wanted to settle deeper and just fall asleep. He pushed the key into the ignition, turned it, and the van fired up easily.

He backed out and around, so that he was facing up the drive toward the gate. He wanted to make loading up the girls and leaving as easy as possible. Backing down the dark drive just felt like it was more hassle than it would be worth.

He pulled up in front of the door, leaving the driveway and driving up over the lawn and the narrow walk leading to gravel drive. Just a few steps from the door to the van, and the girls would all be safe and on their way home, via the Little Rock FBI office.

Joe got out, slid the side door open and turned back to the house. His heart leapt when he saw a shadowy figure standing in the doorway, backlit by light from inside the house. He reached for the pistol in his jacket pocket, had his hand around it, ready to pull it free when a voice said, "The girls were scared. Some think you're another kidnapper. Other one's thought you just left us."

Joe sucked in a deep breath and released it slowly. He did it twice more before speaking. "No. I'm sorry, had to find keys for the van. Let's go in, get everyone ready and get the hell out of here."

The girl backed up, into the light. He saw her face, the dark circles, blood at the corner of her mouth. Her jeans were faded along the thighs, and her t-shirt was ripped on the seam of the right sleeve.

"Okay," she said. "Those dead guys are gross, just so you know."

"Yeah, I didn't want any of you to see that. If you want to go let the other girls know that we'll be leaving in just a few minutes, I'll find some blankets to toss over their bodies, so no one else sees them."

Joe followed the girl back into the house. He stopped in the living room while she moved through to the kitchen and the room of girls.

There was a throw over the back of the couch, and he grabbed that, taking it into the kitchen. He tossed it over Aikman. It wasn't big enough to cover the entire man, so Joe draped it over his head and body, leaving his feet and lower legs sticking out.

He walked back to the girls, said, "One more minute, okay?" He grabbed two blankets, walked back to the kitchen and tossed one over Peavey's body, avoiding looking at it any longer than he had to.

The next cover he hung over Porter's head. He didn't know how it was possible, but in the twenty-some minutes he had been outside, the man still had not died. Just before he tossed the blanket over Porter's face, he looked into the man's eyes and whispered, "You deserve this, and you know it."

Porter's eyes flicked sideways once, and his lips fluttered, as if he wanted to say something. Fresh tears welled and tracked down his face. Joe tossed the blanket over the big man and walked away. He would do his best to leave Porter there, in his mind, but he had a feeling that the big kidnapper would haunt his nightmares for a long time to come.

Joe tromped back to the bedroom, surveying the girls for several seconds, realizing that some if not most of them, wouldn't trust a word he said. He coughed once, clearing his throat, as if preparing for a big speech. "I know you're all pretty scared. I've gotten a van ready, we're going to load up in it and drive for Little Rock, about an hour from here. We uh, can't really trust the local police, so it has to be the FBI office. I know none of you have a reason to trust me, after what you've been through, but I want to get home, just like you. The van is the same one many of you were brought here in. Just understand when you see it, that it'll be the one to get you to safety. I promise you all."

Joe stopped, just watching the girls again. They all seemed reluctant to move, and he felt for them. He singled out the girl who had meet him at the door, who was comforting another girl who was crying softly into her shoulder. "Can you help these girls get motivated and into the van. I'm gonna get some water for everyone, take it out. We need to be gone in the next two minutes."

The girl looked and nodded. "Yeah, okay. I can do that."

"Thanks. Uh, what's your name?"

"Kim. Kim Oberfield."

"Okay, Kim, I'm Joe Pruitt. I'm pretty sure you and the other girls want to get home, I know I do. Let's work together and get out of here."

The girl nodded again. He turned away, heading toward the kitchen to gather water and another soda for the road. He heard Kim say, "Come on girls, move. This guy's gonna help us get out of this shithole. Help each other walk if you have to. I wanna go home."

Even though his jaw and face hurt miserably from the pounding he had taken, a smile tugged at the corners of his mouth. The girl was tougher than she looked.

He found a plastic garbage bag in a drawer next to the sink. Joe pulled the remaining bottles of water and the sodas from the fridge and dumped them in the bag. He didn't know if only one or two or all six of the girls would want the water, and the drive was only an hour, but he'd rather have it with him just in case.

The girls filed past in three pairs, leaning on each other or helping support a weaker girl. Every one of them looked exhausted, miserable. As much as he hurt over his entire body, as utterly fatigued as he was, Joe didn't think he could even imagine what these young girls were feeling. The abuse they had suffered. Not knowing what was happening, but maybe understanding deep inside why they had been taken. Did they know they had been kidnapped to be used for sexual slavery?

No child anywhere should ever have to fear that. Joe felt the anger welling up in him again, and he wanted to lash out, to feel that satisfaction he had felt earlier when putting the bullets into Peavey's chest.

Standing there in the kitchen with the heavy sack of drinks hanging from his hand, Joe glanced around the kitchen once more, at the covered bodies of men he had killed. Tomorrow he might feel remorse at taking not just one, but many human lives. Right now, though, with crying children parading past him, he simply felt justification.

Joe turned, took two steps toward the living

room and stopped. He glanced back once more. Underlying everything, Joe felt that he was missing something, that there was *something* he should be seeing. He probed at the thought, pushed at it like a bad tooth, but nothing would come. It was an uneasy feeling, but one he couldn't put a fact to.

"Fuck it," he muttered to the dead men. As he turned away he caught something out of the corner of his eye and looked back once more.

Sitting on the table that had been shoved across the room, balanced precariously on the edge, sat a laptop computer. Joe had no clue what the men used it for, but if they used it to coordinate their kidnapping and transfers of the girls, it could be invaluable in stopping future abductions. Joe stepped over Aikman's legs and walked to the table. He closed the top of the computer, popped the cord free from the wall with a yank and tucked the device up under his arm. He would take it to the FBI, they might be able to do something with it.

Joe Pruitt walked out of the house, tossed the sack into the van, dropped the computer in the passenger seat and slid the door shut. He then climbed into the driver's seat and said over his shoulder. "Let's get the hell out of here."

Chapter 47

Gravel crunched under the tires as Joe pulled down the driveway. He was careful not to run over Dave's body as he pulled toward the gate. Driving through, he stopped at the intersection of the driveway and the gravel road and pulled the phone from his pocket, bringing up the search information he had found earlier in the night. Using the maps application, Joe plotted a course to the FBI office in Little rock, placed the phone in a mount on the dash, turned left and pulled away.

"We're on our way, girls.

The sounds of soft weeping and whispered talk followed him as he piloted the van into the night, the headlights cutting the darkness from his path.

Chapter 48

The eerie silence of the house was ruptured when Anthony Peavey woke with an inhaled breath and a shout of pain. He was startled by the darkness pressing against his face until he ripped the blanket away, relishing the feel of the cooler air entering his lungs.

His chest and head both throbbed, each seeming to pound to the beat of a different drummer. He pushed himself up into a sitting position and reached for the back of his head. He could feel the edges of the split in the back of his scalp like weird lips. The blood was thick, tacky and matted in his hair.

He tried drawing a deep breath, but his chest felt as if it were on fire from the inside. He unbuttoned his shirt, looking closely at the two holes, one on each side.

Had that bastard shot him while he was unconscious?

The two bullets lodged in the tactical vest beneath his shirt suggested he had. If he hadn't put on the vest, he would be dead right now. Peavey had begun wearing it after a hand-off went bad two years ago, leaving him with a bullet in his side and two of his men dead. Now, any time things looked like they might go south, he would slip it on and wear his shirt over it, so it wasn't obvious that he had protection.

Peavey sat there on the floor for a full two minutes, his legs still covered by the blanket like he was some geriatric invalid that had fallen and was unable to get up. He gazed around the room at the carnage Joe Pruitt had left in his wake. He wasn't so sure the man was untrained, or unskilled. Then again, he hadn't checked to make sure I was dead, Peavey thought.

Why had the man covered him and the others in blankets? There was no reason unless… "The girls!" Peavey shouted. He rolled to the side and got to his knees, then used the counter to pull himself up.

God, that hurts! It felt like there were twin rods of flame buried in his chest. The vest had protected him from the trauma of a penetrating bullet, but the force of the bullet impacting the vest still left deep bruises. Peavey felt like luck had been on his side, that the bullets hadn't impacted directly over his heart, possibly stopping it the way a hard punch could.

Once he was fully upright, Peavey stood with one hand braced on the counter, taking slow, shallow breaths. His vision swam, darkened at the edges and came back several times. He felt dizzy and disoriented. It took him several false starts before he was able to shuffle across the room and down the hall toward the room where they held the girls.

He could see the light was on and that at least two of the beds were empty before he even reached the room. Peavey ran his hand along the undecorated wall of the hallway, keeping himself upright, fighting the dizziness and nausea threatening to overwhelm him. Probably got a damn concussion, he thought. Average Joe, buddy, I get the chance, I'm gonna kill you slow, you...

"Damn it!" Peavey shouted as he moved through the door into the room filled with beds and no girls. Joe had covered the dead men so that the girls wouldn't see as they left they house. "You shithouse bastard!" Peavey shouted into the room. He swooned, weaving in place. He took several breaths, steadied himself, and went back to the kitchen.

Peavey stopped cold, hand still braced on the wall, when he saw the laptop gone from the kitchen table. "No, oh hell no! Damn it! Damn it!"

From under the blanket on the floor, Peavey heard a moan, then Aikman's voice said, "Help me, Peavey."

He stumbled across the room, carefully knelt down next to the man and pulled the cover away. Aikman's eyes rolled to look at him, and Peavey took in the sight of the man's mangled, swollen nose and bleeding stomach. He looked like he had been painted with a wide roller of red, from his face, all the way down to his upper thighs.

Aikman's voice was weak when he said, "Fucker gut-shot me. Can you believe that shit?"

Peavey nodded. "With this guy, I'd believe just about anything at this point. He shot me in the chest. Twice."

Aikman looked confused and Peavey pulled his shirt apart to show the man the vest beneath. "Huh," was Aikman's only response.

219

"We have to go after him. He's got the girls, and my laptop."

"I need a doctor."

"We'll get you one, but if someone gets ahold of that laptop... It's just bad."

Aikman stared at Peavey for a moment then asked, "What's on it?"

"An insurance policy in case Meryl or any one of the people we dealt with ever tried to screw me over. Names, dates, even some pictures."

Aikman coughed once. "Jesus, Peavey." There was little emphasis to his words.

"Yeah, Jesus is right, as in we'll need Jesus if anyone gets their hands on it, and I highly doubt even He would be inclined to help us. Can you get up?"

"My arm."

Peavey looked down, seeing the broken arm for the first time. "Damn, he did a number on you, buddy."

"Yeah. Need a hospital. A doctor." Hospital sounded more like *hozbipal* to Peavey.

Aikman seemed to be fading in and out, and Peavey wasn't willing to waste any more time on the dying man.

"Yeah, I'll get you to a hospital, Andrew. I need the keys for the Camaro."

Looking out across the room, staring into space, Aikman said, "Ruined my car. Said he... did something to the engine, Peavey. My beautiful car." A weak sob escaped along with a bubble of blood.

"We'll make him pay for that, buddy. I promise." Peavey's tone was deceptively conciliatory. "I still need the keys. I want that little arsenal you keep in the trunk."

Aikman's eyes flicked to Peavey then down. "Pocket."

Aikman's scream when Peavey moved his broken arm to get to the pocket made his aching head swim. Stars spun, and galaxies whipped around him for several seconds. The nausea threated to force up what little he had in his stomach.

With keys in hand, Peavey left a weeping Aikman laying on the floor and walked unsteadily out of the kitchen toward the front door, the ground beneath him threatening to pitch him over as it seemed to flow and buckle with every step.

Chapter 49

Joe slapped himself in the face and instantly regretted it. Pain fired across his jaw, wrapped around his skull and seemed to squeeze his brain. Gritting his teeth against the pain, Joe pressed the button that brought the driver's side window down. The cool night air swelled into the cabin of the van and seemed to sooth the raw, screaming nerves of his face.

He had only been driving for ten minutes and already the road and the deep comfortable seat were lulling him, pulling him further into the exhaustion he already felt. The world outside the van had a soft, blurry edge to it.

He tried to speak, and he only squeaked. He cleared his throat and tried again. "Hey, uh, Kim, you still awake back there?"

Silence for several seconds, then the girl was suddenly right beside him, crouching between the seats. He jerked at her surprise appearance. "Yeah?"

"Jeez kid, you scared the crap outta me. Um, in that bag, there were a couple of sodas along with the water. Can you hand me one, please? Need something to help me stay awake."

"Yeah, sure. Hang on." The girl disappeared, ducking into the back of the van. He heard the plastic garbage bag rustling, and another girl asked softly, "What does he want?"

"He just wants a drink," Kim responded.

She was beside him again seconds later,

hand out, holding the sweet soft-drink. "There's one more in the bag. We'll save it for you. Hey, umm, it's a few years yet before I get my license, but I've done some driving, with my Dad. I can drive if you need me to."

Joe smiled. "Thanks, I'll keep that in mind. Might need you too if I can't stay awake. We've got about three miles more on the country roads before we hit paved highway."

"Where did you say we were going?"

"Little Rock. There's an FBI field office there. I figure its safer if we just show up."

"Why safer? Why couldn't you just call the cops or something?"

Joe sighed, and his jaw ached. "Have you been at this house long, or were you at another one tonight, before this one?"

The girl was quite for a moment before answering. "I've been here for three days. A bunch of other girls showed up earlier tonight. I was mostly out of it then, but I still remember that."

"Well, they were moved here because of me. At the house they were at before, I saw those guys pay off a cop, a Sheriff I think. The guy was taking money to just let them move girls through the county. I don't want to risk them having someone else on the payroll. I figure if we just show up at the FBI office, then there's less of a chance that someone's on the take."

"How do you know the FBI people aren't getting money from them too?"

Joe nodded. The girl was quick. "I don't."

"Oh, okay." The girl was silent for a moment, then said, "Well, step on it, Joe. I wanna go home."

Joe could hear the scared little girl in her voice. "Sure thing, Kim. I'll get you there, or at least to the FBI, who'll get you home. I promise."

Kim said nothing and disappeared. Over the wind from the window, and the crunch of gravel beneath the tires, Joe could hear the girls whispering. One of them said "I'm cold" so softly he almost missed it.

Joe pressed the button and brought the window up, leaving only a two-inch gap. He cracked open the bottle of soda, took three deep pulls from the bottle and recapped it, setting it in the cup-holder in the console in front of him.

Joe called over his shoulder, "Hey, uh, you girls mind if I turn on the radio?"

A whispered conversation, then Kim, from the back, said, "That's fine, Mr. Joe. Just nothing old, or dumb."

The smile tugging at the corners of Joe's mouth hurt. He tapped the radio power button and began searching for a station with music that wasn't old or dumb. He didn't care what they listened to, he just wanted the noise.

One mile further, Joe slowed, clicked the turn signal in the direction the map on the phone indicated and the van bounced as it bumped from gravel road to paved highway. There were no other vehicles in sight in either direction.

The GPS showed fifty-two minutes to the

FBI office in Little Rock.

"You got this," he muttered to himself as he clicked on the high-beams, "not much longer now."

Chapter 50

Inside the barn, Peavey leaned against the back of the Camaro and took a minute to take several deep breaths. His chest hurt like hell. His head throbbed. He even entertained the idea that his hair was sending jolts of pain along his scalp. Once the barn stopped spinning around him, he popped the trunk open.

Aikman had bragged to him before about the guns he kept in the trunk of the car. Not because they needed them, but because the man enjoyed having them along. There were two handguns, a long-rifle, two shotguns, and a full-auto FN P90.

Aikman had boasted that he had gotten the short, oddly curvy bullpup type rifle in trade for a girl that the original buyer had backed out on at the last minute. He hadn't given Peavey any specifics, but it sounded like something Aikman would do.

He checked the top-loading magazine and racked the charging handle. The weapon was fully loaded. He took it, and one of the shotguns to the front of the car and dropped them in the front seat, along with a box of ammunition for the shotgun, and three spare magazines for the automatic, then went around and popped the hood. He wanted to see what damage Joe had done to the engine.

He was only mildly surprised to find that nothing had been done to the car other than the fork sticking out of the back window. Peavey slammed the hood, wincing at the noise.

He shuffled around the vehicle. He closed the trunk, went to the driver's side and dropped into the front seat. The engine started up with a roar when he turned the key, and, like many people, Peavey enjoyed the smooth, low rumble of the powerful engine. He didn't consider himself a "car guy" but he could appreciate a great machine.

He pulled the door closed without slamming it, avoiding the crash inside his skull. Peavey backed out of the barn and made a five-point turn, pointing the car down the driveway. He parked in front of the door and sat there staring at the house for several minutes before stepping out of the car. He left the car running and went back inside.

Aikman looked up at him when he walked back into the room. "I hear my car?"

"Yeah. Didn't do anything to the engine. He probably just said that to piss you off." Peavey glanced down at Aikman's bleeding abdomen. "Looks like it worked."

Aikman coughed a bubble of blood and tried to push himself up with his good arm. More dark blood welled from the hole in his stomach. "Help me," he groaned, "hospital."

Peavey just watched. When Aikman collapsed back against the wall with a broken sob, Peavey said, "That shit you tried to play with Meryl tonight? All your "yes ma'am" bullshit, trying to make me look bad. Well, fuck you, Andrew."

Peavey took a shuffling half-step forward,

raised his foot and stomped on Aikman's stomach. Blood spurted up through the hole in the man's abdomen, dousing Peavey's shoe.

Aikman leaned forward, spitting blood and screams as Peavey moved around him and kicked his shattered arm, then stomped the broken joint. Bones cracked, and snapped, grinding together as Peavey put all his weight on the arm.

Aikman tried to grab at Peavey's leg with his unbroken arm, but he was too weak to do anything other than a few faint slaps.

Peavey grinned down at the man, raised his foot and slammed it down once more on the crushed joint of Aikman's arm.

Aikman fell over, on his side, away from the pain, his screams breaking, becoming uncontrollable sobs.

Peavey moved away from the man and bent over with his hands on his knees, sucking air, willing the room to stop spinning. Aikman's screams and sobs were like drill-bits boring deep into his brain. Standing upright, he moved away from the sound, toward the front door.

He left it open as he walked back out to the car. Inside, he rolled the window down, put the car into drive and pulled away. He slowed at the intersection of the driveway and road, and he could still hear intermittent screams coming from the house. He looked both directions and pulled out onto the gravel road.

I'm coming for you, Joe, he thought.

Chapter 51

Joe swerved, and the tires rumbled as they passed over the strip along the edge of the road, doing what they were intended to, jerking his attention back to the road, and not the backs of his drifting eyelids.

He pinched his nose, rubbed at his gritty eyes, and ground his teeth. The pain from his jaw served to jolt him awake a little more, but even that was quickly losing its effect. He was simply exhausted, but he was determined to get the girls to the FBI office. After that, he would sleep for a week.

He took a long pull from the soda, recapped it and placed it back in the holder. "Hey, ladies, huddle up a little okay? I need to roll the window down a bit more."

Mutterings and whispers came from the back, then Kim said from behind his seat, "Go ahead, Mr. Joe."

Joe lowered the window half-way, hoping to find a happy medium that would keep cold air on his face and not send too much into the back of the van. He groaned audibly and said, "Okay, stop with the "Mr. Joe" stuff. Sounds like a character from a really bad movie. Joe is fine, or Mr. Pruitt, though I can't say I favor that much more than I do Mr. Joe." Joe affected a silly, exaggerated super-hero voice and said, "Or you can call me Captain Average! He gets the job done."

A faint chuckle and several groans came from the back. A voice said, "Great, Dad jokes."

It hurt to smile, but Joe couldn't help himself.

Kim had become the spokesman for the group of girls, and to Joe it seemed to come naturally for her. She said, "That's right, you said you had a daughter. What's she like?"

Joe stared out the windshield, thinking. He must have gone silent for too long.

"Joe?" Kim asked.

"Yeah. Uh, well, Cady Lynn is nine, going on ten-years-old. Light brown hair like her momma's. Kind of a skinny kid, real athletic, likes to run. I didn't get to take her as much as I would have liked, but she loved fishing. Biggest, most beautiful dang smile I've ever seen. She giggles a lot, like she knows a joke you just aren't in on. She's a great kid."

For a moment, the knot that returned to Joe's chest and rose into his throat hurt more than his split nose, aching jaw, or even the bullet wound in his shoulder. Tears pooled in his eyes, and no matter how hard he fought to keep them back, they fell anyway. His chest hitched as he resisted a sob. He knew that he would start crying soon, and that was the last thing this bunch of girls needed. Besides, how bad were things for him, really, compared to what they had gone through.

"Hey, Joe."

"Yeah, what's up, Kim?"

"It sounds like, you know, she's not around

anymore. Did she, you know, uh…?"

Joe's brow creased for a second, then he realized what she meant. He had been speaking of his daughter in the past-tense. Sometimes, that's how it felt, as if he might never see her again. "No, she's not dead. Her mom and I got divorced a while back, they moved out to California with my Ex's new husband. Haven't seen her in far too long. But, to be honest, going a day without seeing my daughter is far too long."

"Why don't you move to California?"

Joe chuckled. "I've been asking myself the same thing, Kimmy."

The girl groaned loudly behind his seat. "Oh, God, don't call me Kimmy, please."

This time Joe's laugh was genuine, coming from his belly. "Sure thing, Kim. Sorry," he said wearing his painful grin.

Joe glanced down at the phone when the GPS app directed him to make a right turn in one-hundred yards. He was coming up on the small town of Center Ridge. From there he would get on highway 92 and follow that to Interstate 40, which would take him all the way to Little Rock.

The tiny town was still sound asleep at almost 4:30 in the morning. They were through it in minutes, and Joe turned onto 92, the road smoother than any had been on yet. He thought they must have resurfaced it recently.

Joe pushed on, gripping the wheel tightly, the van falling back into silence. He thought he heard a couple of the girls snoring softly. He hoped they could sleep. It was all he wanted to do at that very moment and he was envious. He wondered if sleeping might be a defense mechanism, a way to just avoid the whole night, and hopefully wake up to a new and better day. Or it could be the residual effect of the drugs they had been forced to take. Either way, sleep sounded good to him.

He pressed down on the gas pedal, and the van surged forward. He watched the needle climb and he leveled it off at seventy miles an hour. Joe prayed that the cops were elsewhere tonight, watching another road, because he was determined not to stop for anyone or anything until they were in front of the Little Rock FBI office.

He imagined a line of police cars chasing him, lights flashing, bull horns blaring at him to pull over and exit the van. The thought of it made his skin crawl. It would be a low speed chase because he wasn't about to drive like a madman with these girls in the van. They would probably try to set up a road block, stop him with force if they had too.

He left off the accelerator and let it drift down to sixty-five. No matter how fast he drove, even if he got to Little Rock in the next ten minutes, it wouldn't be soon enough.

Suddenly, Joe felt a yawn creeping up on him. Oh, God, no, he thought. But once a yawn was begun, there was no stopping it until it was done. His mouth opened, his jaw cracking the wider it got. Pain flared across his face, radiating out in every direction at once. He couldn't suppress the weak sob that came out with the yawn.

"Joe, you ok?"

His mouth closed, and he swiped at the tear running down his bruised face. "I'm okay, Kim. You just rest, we'll be there soon."

Joe glanced at the rearview mirror. He could see little in the back of the dark van, and with the windows blacked out, there was nothing behind. He flicked his eyes to the wide side-mirror, checking out of habit.

It could be an early riser from Center Ridge, heading to work, but the headlights behind him made his heart jump in his chest before he remembered that he had killed anyone who might pursue them.

Get used to being paranoid, he thought to himself as he focused on the road ahead. Joe reached for his soda, took a swig and drove on into the dark.

Chapter 52

Peavey stopped at the intersection where the gravel met blacktop and took a moment to think. Where would he be going if he were an average Joe asshole who had rescued a bunch of kidnapped girls, but didn't trust local authorities?

The FBI? Understanding law-enforcement, where they were and how they worked was part of what Peavey did. He knew the two closest offices were in Little Rock and Memphis. The next three would be St. Louis, Oklahoma City, and Jackson, all of which he thought would be too far.

He was sure Joe was exhausted, hurt, scared. He would want this done as soon as possible, get the girls safe and get himself some medical care. Little Rock it was. He was working on assumptions, but it was all he had at this point. The guy was most likely using GPS on his stolen phone. He would be following a set route and keeping his speed down. The last thing Joe would want is to be pulled over in the middle of nowhere, so he would avoid all reasons to be stopped.

Peavey didn't care about being stopped, his only concern was getting the laptop back at this point and killing the son-of-a-bitch Joe Pruitt. Even the girls no longer mattered to him. If he couldn't collect them, he would at least make sure they didn't talk to anyone, ever. He checked the FN P90, took the weapon off safe and sat it in the seat next to him.

Deep breaths hurt, but Peavey drew one in anyway. Then a second one. His head was already swimming in a distorted sea of pain and shallow breathing wasn't helping matters any.

He lifted his foot from the brake, pressed down on the accelerator and the car roared as it threw a high tail of loose gravel into the air before shooting out onto the pavement.

Tires squealed as Peavey pulled at the wheel, bringing the car around and rocketing into the night. To Peavey it felt like the deep rumble wasn't coming from the powerful engine, but from inside his skull and vibrating out. He worked against the dizziness and throbbing pain; focusing on the road ahead, and how much pleasure he would get from shooting that bastard in the face.

Peavey pressed the pedal down, quickly bringing the car up to ninety, then one-hundred miles per hours. The tires sung on the smooth pavement. With the window down, using the cool air to help keep him focused, Peavey slowed at curves, then brought the car back up to speed. On open, straight road, he pushed it up to one-twenty. The feeling of the world whipping past so quickly was a rush he hadn't expected.

At the moment he was operating on guess-work, hoping this was the route Joe had taken toward Little Rock. He couldn't be sure, but he felt confident this is the way he would have come. Peavey had driven these roads many times over the past few years with van-loads of girls and young women, as well as the occasional soccer-mom or corporate type. He worked to fill the requests that Meryl sent him from the buyers. It didn't matter to him what they wanted. He provided a service and made damn good money doing it.

Most of the grabs were fairly simple, a little planning, a little waiting, then toss them into the van and get out. Chloroform for the initial knock-out, drugs to keep them docile until they were handed off to the buyer or someone who would be transporting them across the country or out of it to their final destination.

He wished, right then, that Mike and David were still alive, so he could beat them to death for their unplanned grab of the girl in Jonesboro. Every one of them had taken a girl when the opportunity arose, even in broad daylight, it happened, though not very often due to the risk involved. This had been one time they should have kept driving.

Peavey gritted his teeth at a sharp sting of pain from the back of his head. He hadn't taken the time to bandage it, and the wound throbbed at the chill air bursting through the window. He powered on through the night, eyes drilling through the dark, hoping to see taillights ahead.

Several minutes later, Peavey passed a sign indicating that he was near Center Ridge. Where from here? He thought. South on 92, most likely. Going through the small town, he slowed the car to eighty miles an hour. As soon as he hit the edge of town, and he made the turn onto 92, he dropped his foot and the car shot forward.

Not long after that twin red eyes appeared in the darkness ahead. Taillights. They were barely discernable, and they could belong to someone heading in to work early, or even a cop. Peavey snarled at the windshield, pushed down on the gas pedal, and the car climbed from one-hundred to one-twenty in a hurry. The lights drew rapidly closer, and he was confident that it was the van, his van.

"Got you now, shithead," Peavey growled. He reached over and pulled the short rifle closer, resting it between the seats. The pain in his head and chest was briefly forgotten. He was high on the hunt, and his prey was close.

Then the dark stillness of the night around him was suddenly torn open by light and sound. A wailing siren, flashing red and blue lights coming from behind and to the left, out of a little side area cut into some trees along the highway.

Peavey jerked the gun into his lap. Nothing was going to prevent him from reaching Joe Pruitt.

Chapter 53

Joe glanced at the side mirror again, watching the headlights. They seemed to be growing, rapidly getting closer. He tried to push the paranoid thoughts of pursuit aside, but he was unable to shake them entirely. Just someone running late for their morning shift, he thought, unconvincingly.

The highway droned on in front of him, and he checked the road, then glanced back at the mirror once more. Lights burst into an oddly cheerful display behind him, behind the other vehicle. "Damn. Sorry, buddy, you're gonna be late anyway," he muttered.

"What?" Kim not Kimmy asked from the back.

"Oh, nothing. There was a car back there, looked to be moving pretty fast. I think it just got pulled over."

"A car behind us? You don't think...?" The tension in her voice was unmistakable, and the other girls started to babble fearful questions.

Joe did think, but he knew better. He knew what he'd done. There was no way. "No. I... uh, made sure they wouldn't be coming after us." I think I did. He remembered the uneasy feeling he had in the kitchen, like he was missing something. He had forcibly dismissed it then. It wasn't as easy to do now, with the lights behind them.

In the mirror, the headlights and the swirling

reds and blues continued to grow closer. Whoever it was, they weren't stopping for the cop car.

Joe accelerated, moving up to seventy-five, then past that to eighty when the lights behind continued to come closer. Joe could feel the speed of the vehicle in the way it rocked and swayed. The big van wasn't made to cruise at high speeds. The girl's chattering grew louder.

The miles flew by in a hurry, and the twenty from Center Ridge to the tiny burg of Plumerville shrunk until only minutes later, Joe saw a sign at the same time the GPS informed him that he would be making a left turn onto 40 South toward Conway and Little Rock.

He had no idea what was happening behind him, but the lights were almost close enough to touch. He could hear the police siren over the rush of the wind and the tire noise on the roadway. He could also hear the deep rumble of the car between the police car and the van. The kind of rumble only a classic muscle car could make. Like a restored '67 Camaro.

Joe glanced down at the needle. It was edging up between eighty-five and ninety now. The van felt like a tiny boat on rough seas, rocking hard with the irregularities of the road. There was no way he could risk pushing it higher.

Then the lights behind him were right there and moving into the lane next to him. He glanced at the mirror, but the bright light reflected from the other car's headlights blinded him to everything until the rumbling vehicle was right next to him.

The phone let him know that his turn was coming up. He barely heard it over the girl's talking.

He turned his head to look out the side window, at the other vehicle. The red and blue lights flashing from behind cast an eerie fluctuating glow inside the Camaro next to him. He could make out an odd-looking gun being pointed in his direction, and the grinning face of Peavey behind it, his other hand on the wheel.

Joe's brow creased. How? He had shot Peavey twice in the chest. There was no way the man was still alive. It was a question for another time. Right now, there were more immediate concerns.

Joe jerked the wheel away from Peavey and the gun on instinct alone, reacting to the situation without thought. The van seemed to shudder in protest as is shifted over, as if it disliked moving so quickly at such high speeds. Joe knew he didn't like it either.

The gun chattered, and a short stream of bullets plunked into the top edge of his door. The girls screamed, and Joe swore at the sudden violent burst. He forced his eyes forward, to watch the road. His turn was coming. Little Rock was getting closer.

The overpass he would have to go under to make the left turn to 40 was just ahead, he could see it, but with Peavey and the Camaro on his left he knew there was no way he would make it.

Peavey would shoot him or push him over before he could get there.

Joe looked at the signs, took a moment to think, and let off the gas pedal. The Camaro shot forward, followed closely by the police car, its siren blaring. The speedometer hit seventy and Joe risked a hard right turn onto the exit ramp for 40 going in the opposite direction. For a heartbeat, Joe thought the van might tilt and go over. The girls must have thought so as well, because they screamed again with the sudden shift.

He focused on the road ahead and accelerated, pushing the van as hard as he dared, putting as much distance between him and the Camaro as was possible. He had no doubt Peavey would try to come back for him, he prayed the cop could somehow stop the crazy kidnapper.

Chapter 54

Peavey spat curses at the windshield as he dropped the rifle in the seat and placed both hands on the wheel. With the cop car right behind him, he couldn't slam on the brakes and make the turn he needed to.

He shot under the overpass. Peavey wanted to haul the car hard to the right and cut back up the exit lane, but the cop was just too close. Instead, he opted to pull his foot off the pedal and let the car slow naturally. Half a mile later, he was able to hit the right turn onto 64. He was still moving at high speed, and the tires protested violently at the abuse, but he was able to keep the skid under control and pull the car straight and steady once more.

He was now moving straight through the tiny heart of the village of Plumerville. At 5 a.m. the town was still fast asleep. The cop shot past the turn, but Peavey knew he would be back. He dropped the pedal and accelerated again. This road intersected with 113/AR-9 a couple miles ahead, at Morrilton. If Joe was intent on getting to Little Rock, like he believed, then he would have to take AR-9 south at Morrilton. Peavey could catch him there.

Two minutes later the flashing lights of the cop car appeared in his rearview mirror. He would have to do something about the cop.

Chapter 55

Daniel Lucas was sitting back, relaxed, in the seat of his car, backed into his favorite spot to watch for early morning speeders when the van went by. He was using his phone to plan out his upcoming three-day-weekend.

His wife was flying out to see her sister in Tucson, and he and his son were planning on spending all three days camping and fishing at Lake Ouachita.

At eleven years old, it wasn't always easy to get Kevin interested in something other than video games and his cell phone, so Daniel had been a little surprised at how excited the boy had gotten over the prospect of spending three whole days out on the lake.

Daniel had the window down, enjoying the early morning silence. He considered this his favorite part of the day. The roads were usually quiet, he was only a couple of hours from the end of his shift and he was ready to head home. He would see Kevin off to school, his wife would leave for work a few minutes after that and Daniel would get some sleep.

When he had heard a vehicle coming, he glanced up at his console. The van was moving just a few miles over the speed-limit. He let it go. Probably some small-time delivery driver trying to make up a few minutes in the early morning hours when the road was clear and quiet.

A minute later he heard the rumble of

another vehicle approaching. With that kind of noise, he guessed it was an older vehicle, souped-up, a real powerhouse under the hood.

The car cruised by and his dash unit went off with its alarm. The readout read one-hundred twenty-two. He tossed his phone into the passenger seat, hit the lights and siren at the same time he shouted "Jesus!" at the windshield. It went by so fast that he couldn't identify the vehicle.

Dirt and rocks flew from under his tires as he tore out from his parking spot, bumped up onto the paved roadway from the short dirt track and pulled the heavy cruiser around with a squeal of rubber.

Daniel called the pursuit in to dispatch, detailing location and speed. He would update with vehicle make and plate number as soon as he was able.

The car was already far ahead of him, and he tromped the pedal, pushing his on car up to it's limits in a hurry. Even after the years of defensive and offensive driving courses, he'd never been entirely comfortable with high-speed pursuits. Too many variables, too much risk. Occasionally it was part of the job, though, and he took his job seriously.

He began to gain on the speeder, inches at a time, and was soon close enough to pull the plate number and relay that info.

Maybe a mile ahead, Daniel glimpsed taillights. The van. Was the speeder chasing the van? It was a thought, and there was little time to process it as they came upon the larger vehicle.

Daniel was able to push close, get a make and model on the car, and verify there was only one occupant. The back glass was shattered with an oblong hole in the center of the window, about twelve inches long and three inches wide. The shattered glass made it difficult to see much inside the car, but it was obvious when the driver raised something in his hand, pointing it toward the van.

Daniel knew, seconds before he heard it, that it would be an automatic weapon. Probably some sort of machine pistol.

The van swerved to the right at the last possible second, and he thought that probably saved the driver's life. The rapid *brackckacka* of the weapon was absorbed into the rumble of the Camaro and the rushing of the wind, all of it creating a dissonant cacophony that grated instantly on Daniel's nerves.

The early morning had changed, from sudden speeder to unexpected violence. Gripping the rocking steering wheel tightly with his left hand, he keyed his mic and informed dispatch of the automatic weapons fire.

Being a small-town police officer didn't mean Daniel wasn't trained to handle unusual violent scenarios, it just meant that is was uncommon. As he piloted the car down the road, backing off and giving the Camaro a little room, so that he wouldn't rear-end it if the guy slammed on his brakes, he pushed aside all thoughts of fishing and family and focused on his job.

Questions arose. Who was in the van? Why was the driver of the Camaro shooting at them? Was it a drug-deal gone wrong? Angry husband chasing his wife's lover?

They were coming up on Plumerville fast, and he needed to make a decision on how to proceed.

Seconds later, part of that decision was made for him when the big van suddenly pulled right and shot up the exit lane to 40. It looked for a moment like the big vehicle would tilt, maybe tip, but it stayed steady and rocketed up the lane. Good driving, he thought.

Daniel refocused on the Camaro in front and planned out how to stop the speeding shooter.

Chapter 56

Joe's heart was pounding, and the adrenaline coursing through his veins was deadening his pains for the moment. He was also wide awake now.

He barley heard the GPS directing him to reroute over the girl's crying and chatter. Two miles ahead he would have to exit the highway and get on 9/113 if he wanted to get to Little Rock. The distance was longer on this route, and the time had jumped from just under fifty minutes to just over an hour, now. But that was only if he were driving the speed limit.

Joe had no idea where the Camaro had gone, but he hoped to be long down the road before it ever found them again.

The two miles to his exit and the town of Morrilton were gone in minutes. He made the exit, slowing enough to execute the turns without feeling like the van was going to tip over. As he pulled out from an intersection, onto Route 9, Joe said, "Girls?" He raised his voice to be heard over their din. "Hey girls, I need you all to take a breath and sit tight. Were on a different route now, it might take a bit longer, but we'll get there."

"Joe, who was that? Did we lose them?"

"It was one of the guys from the house. Honestly, Kim, I thought I'd, you know, killed them all. I don't understand it. One guy was shot in the stomach, dying. The other guy," Joe didn't want to share the graphic details, so he said, "was already dead. And I shot their leader in the chest, twice. There's no way he could have survived."

From behind his seat, the girl said, "Maybe he was wearing a bullet-proof vest."

Joe's brow wrinkled, and even though he had heard her he said, "What?"

"You know, like cops and Army guys wear."

"Yeah, I know what a vest is, I just..." Joe went silent as he guided the van down the road.

His eyes saw the road ahead, but he thought back to the kitchen, to the bodies of the men he killed. He remembered shooting Peavey in the chest, the feel of the pistol going off, the look of the bullets hitting the man's white shirt. In his memory he could see Peavey's body jump with the impact of the bullets.

Joe stepped through every move he had made. Getting water for the girls, clearing the gate, searching for the keys. He had gotten the van and parked it in front of the house. Blankets and dropping them over the bodies of the dead men. Peavey with the two holes in his white shirt.

The white shirt.

"Oh, God," Joe moaned.

Chapter 57

The turn for 113 came up fast, and Peavey dropped his speed to make the loop around the exit ramp. He would have preferred to wait here, where he was certain Joe would be passing any minute now, but with the cop on his tail, it wasn't possible.

He pulled through the long turn and hit the gas again as soon as he was pointed down the straight-away, the signs for 9/113 guiding the way. The cop had taken the long curve around the exit loop more carefully and it took him a moment to catch up.

Peavey knew he needed to do something about the cop, and soon. Joe and the van full of his girls should be coming down the road any minute, and he wanted to be ready for them.

Maybe I can make this work, he thought, as he powered down the highway. If he was in front of Joe, it might be easier to force him to slow down, get him to stop. Then he could just step out of the car, unload a magazine into the van, get his laptop and disappear.

Meryl would be pissed about the girls. She would be even angrier if she knew what was on the computer. The loss of men meant nothing to that woman. She would replace them by tomorrow. Now that he thought about it, the deaths of his crew meant nothing to Peavey as well.

At least she had taken the three special

orders. Each of those three were worth as much as the other girls combined.

Call her once Joe's dead, try to sort it out. If it sounded like she would rather dispose of him, he would simply disappear. With his laptop full of secrets.

First, he had to stop this cop, then Joe.

Chapter 58

Daniel pulled hard around the loop and shoved down on the pedal, hoping to catch up to the Camaro. It was just over a mile to the bridge spanning the Arkansas River. Beyond that, around what locals called Sequoia Curve, was the small town of Oppelo. He wanted to stop the car at the bridge, before the big curve, well before it went plowing through the small sleeping town.

Whatever was under the Camaro's hood was strong. Daniel glanced at his speedometer. He was pushing one-hundred miles per hour. Far too fast for comfort. The Camaro was still pulling away. He swore at the windshield when it disappeared around a curve.

The road angled back the other direction, just past that curve, leading to the bridge. Even though he wanted to tromp down and attempt to gain on the car, he couldn't bring himself to go any faster, not around even the long curves.

Less than two minutes later, Daniel Lucas rounded the curve that lead straight to the narrow two-lane bridge. He could see that the water was up. He had seen the Arkansas River when it was this high many times over the years. It always looked like hot chocolate to him, dark and murky. He used to tease Kevin, ask the boy if he wanted a cup-full. It always elicited a goofy giggle, and a "No way, Dad, fish pee in that!"

Daniel hit the bridge at eighty miles and

hour, and instantly realized that the Camaro was stopped just on the other side of the bridge, it's red taillights glaring at him through the darkness.

He tapped the brakes, but he was already half-way across when the man stepped out of the Camaro and faced his direction. The interior light from the vehicle silhouetted his form in the night. Daniel could see the shape shift, move as it raised something in its hands.

The automatic weapon. He hammered the brake, standing on it, as if trying to bring the car to an instant stand-still by willpower alone.

Muzzle-flashes in darkness. The ripping sound of the gun. Bullets thunked into the hood and raked up the windshield. The car began to spin as Daniel jerked the wheel in a moment of panic.

The vehicle turned, tires squealing, and bullets flew through the open window. He was stitched across the chest, face and shoulder with white-hot bullets. Part of his lower jaw disintegrated with the impact of a slug.

He jerked the wheel back the other way, reacting, and nothing more. Pain swelled within him, overtaking everything. The tires caught, the car began to tilt, then it was up in the air, rolling as it crashed back to the ground. Daniel Lucas was nothing but a bleeding rag-doll inside the car. It flipped three times, side over side until it came to rest on its front wheels, propped up with the trunk of the cruiser jutting out over the concrete and metal rail along the left side of the bridge.

Daniel was over the steering-wheel, pressed against the windshield, his broken left leg hanging from the driver's window, his right pressed against the seat behind him. Blood ran from the missing portion of his jaw and created a small bloody lake along the dashboard.

He was unable to draw a full breath, and with the last bit of air in his punctured lungs, he sobbed his son's name and died.

Chapter 59

The smells of gasoline, and hot rubber wafted down the bridge toward him, and Peavey grinned at the sight of the car as it flipped through the air several times and came to a stop propped on the bridge railing.

He wanted to run up and make sure the cop was dead. Unload another full magazine into both cop and car. But, he had to move. He didn't want to be sitting right here when Joe showed up, or anyone else for that matter.

Most drivers would see the wrecked police cruiser and make a phone call or stop to see if the officer was injured. Joe would see it as a warning. Peavey knew if he was out here in the open where Joe could see him, he would just turn the van around and go another direction.

Peavey climbed back into the idling Camaro. He took a moment to replace the spent magazine before setting the gun in the seat next to him.

He pulled away from the bridge, glancing back in the side mirror, smiling again at his handiwork with the police car.

"You're next, Average Joe," he muttered as he drove, looking for the best place to set up an ambush for the van and the man behind the wheel.

Chapter 60

Joe wanted to smack himself in the face. Not because he was tired, not to wake up and focus on driving. He wanted to slap himself out of anger, for missing the most obvious sign that Peavey wasn't dead back at the house.

There had been no blood on the shirt. It was something that had registered only in the back of his mind, which, at the time, had been focused on ten different things at once. Now, thinking back, it was clear as day what his sub-conscious had been trying to tell him. Seasoned combat vets and trained detectives wouldn't have missed it. The mistake was further proof that even though he had somehow survived the night so far, he was far out of his league.

Joe glanced at the GPS map on the cell phone. It was about four curvy miles to the Arkansas River. Zooming out, it looked like the twisting route passed through a number of small towns before reaching Little Rock.

Following the normal speed limit, he would be there in just under an hour. Joe wasn't about to follow the speed limit. He suspected that there would be other police officers responding to any call that the driver of the cruiser had put in to his dispatch. Joe didn't plan on stopping for them or anyone else.

They were all probably decent cops, but he had also believed that the cop who had shown up at the first house was there to help, until he saw the man take money to look the other way while Peavey and his crew trafficked girls through his county. It had sounded like he had been doing so for a while. He had been familiar and easy with Peavey, not nervous or intimidated.

His mind was set. He would stop the van at the gates of the FBI office in Little Rock and not before that.

Not for anyone.

Chapter 61

Peavey slowed the Camaro, keeping his speed below seventy. Joe was coming, he was certain of it. It was just a waiting game now. He drove through several small towns, watching for the best location to wait.

Almost seventeen miles later, Peavey pulled up to Will's Junction, a small filling station at a Y intersection. The road branched here, with AR-9 continuing south, and AR-10 going east, toward Little Rock. Pruitt would stay on AR-10.

Peavey sat in the rumbling car, watching the area around him. He glanced at his watch, closing in on 6 a.m. Lights appeared in the distance, coming toward him along AR-10. It was the wrong direction for Joe to be approaching from. A minute later an old, beat-up pickup truck lumbered by.

Peavey stepped out of the car, watching the truck drive away. He walked up to the door of the convenience store and checked the sign stuck to the inside of the door with little suction-cups. 8 a.m. to 8 p.m.

He had a little time before the owner or manager showed up to open the store, but he was uncomfortable sitting out in front of the shop. Back inside the Camaro, he drove around the building, finding the perfect spot to wait.

A narrow service lane that connected the two arms of the Y ran behind the store and the pumps. Peavey drove around the building once more. The area behind the building couldn't be seen by anyone approaching from the north along AR-9.

He moved back behind the building, parked on the paved path and left the car idling as the sun began to peek over the horizon. He did his best to ignore his exhaustion, the pain in his head and chest, and the blurry edges of his vision.

Joe was coming. He had to be ready.

Chapter 62

Joe saw the car on the bridge and slowed to ten miles an hour as he drew close. It was a police cruiser, its rear end hanging over the railing. Chunks of the car and pieces of glass littered the bridge around it. Joe felt guilty that his first concern was that he didn't puncture a tire.

He couldn't be certain, but he believed it was the car that had been chasing Peavey. It was the only thing that made any sense. Which meant Peavey was somewhere on the road ahead.

Maybe he turned back, looking for me, Joe thought. The bullet holes along the front of the car and the windshield made Joe's gut ache. He felt somehow responsible for the cop's death, and he was certain the man was dead. He could see a shadowed, unmoving shape tossed over the steering wheel.

He wanted to get out and check, to be certain, but his mission now was to get the girls to Little Rock, and he was adamant that he wouldn't stop for anyone or anything until he got them there, safe and alive. As much as he hated to do it, Joe pressed on the gas, and the van rolled past the wreck.

If the officer had called in the pursuit, others may show up at any minute. Once across the bridge, Joe glanced at the side mirror, watching the car for a moment. "Sorry, buddy" he murmured.

Joe accelerated, bringing the van back up to sixty-five. He considered the road ahead, and that Peavey may be waiting along it. Peavey having turned around and gone searching for him was wishful thinking and he knew it, but it was too late to turn back now. He didn't believe it would serve any purpose, other than to delay reaching the FBI as soon as possible. It was all guessing. His only plan was to get to the FBI office. To do that he had to drive, just drive.

He was so far beyond tired, and hurting so much, that he just wanted to sleep. Close his eyes and wake up next month, pain free and well rested, with this nightmare long behind him. Joe knew he wasn't thinking as clearly as he should.

He reached out and grabbed the Coke, swigging the last of it just as he came upon a long left-hand curve. He chucked the empty bottle into the footwell of the passenger's seat and followed the curve, passing a sign for the town of Oppelo.

He kept the van's speed low until he reached the other side of the village, then he pressed hard on the pedal and brought the vehicle up to seventy-five quickly. Go. Drive. Little Rock. Girls. Peavey. Hurry. Every thought was a broken piece of another thought, each unformed, exhaustion and pain clouding Joe's thinking.

No matter where this road led, he was on it until he was done, and the girls were safe. If Peavey got in his way, he would deal with him, until then, he drove.

Joe rested his hand on his jacket pocket,

feeling the shape of the pistol beneath the fabric. The pistol was little comfort, not with Peavey's automatic weapon.

The van drifted and the rumble-strip along the shoulder once again jerked Joe back into the moment. The girls in the back got a little louder with the noise, and Kim said, "Joe, you ok up there?"

Rubbing his face with one hand, while holding the wheel with the other, Joe mumbled, "Yeah, Kim. Tired, but I'll make it. Is there any water left?"

The plastic garbage bag rustled. "Yeah, a few."

"Can you pass me one up, please"

Seconds later the girl appeared at his side, holding a bottle of water in front of his face. He took the bottle and glanced at the girl. Her soft features, disheveled hair hanging down over her sleepy face. Joe suddenly missed his daughter with a force that was almost physically painful. He felt a nearly overwhelming urge to weep, hard, uncontrollably, just let it all come out. Joe clenched his aching jaw and the pain was sharp enough to cut through the exhaustion and mental confusion.

Let me get home, God, he thought.

"Thanks."

"Joe?"

"Yeah?" His voice was heavy and even he could hear the pain and sadness in it.

"Don't take this wrong, but…"

"But what?" he asked around a swig of

water.

"You look like poop, Joe."

The girls' comment was so unexpected, Joe spit a mouthful of water over the steering wheel when the laugh burst from his chest. He couldn't help it.

With a grin that hurt from ear to ear he said, "Gee, thanks kid. You look like you could use some sleep. Why don't you go stretch out back there and rest for a few? We should be there in about forty-five minutes."

Every time he spoke to Kim, or the group of girls in general, he had to force his voice to stay calm. He wanted to reassure them that everything was going to be okay with the tone of his voice, even though he was terrified that he wouldn't be able to get them all the way to the FBI safely.

He knew Peavey was either ahead of them or behind, one or the other, and Joe was certain the man had revenge on his mind. He was heading toward a confrontation or running from one.

Peavey might even try to kill the girls out of spite, he could always get more. He obviously had no problem shooting into the van. There was no more concern that he might harm the merchandise.

Chapter 63

Peavey moaned as he shifted in the seat. His head hurt, and his chest ached miserably. The vest may have saved him, but the blunt force of the bullets went deep. Be feeling that for weeks, he thought.

He realized he had been slipping down in the seat and he sat up straighter. If he did have a concussion, the last thing he wanted to do was fall asleep. He imagined the van cruising by while he was passed out behind the wheel, Joe completely unaware that he was there. Peavey could see the man pulling up to the FBI office or police station in Little Rock, turning over the girls and the laptop computer. Everything would be undone, completely and permanently.

Peavey slammed a palm against the steering wheel and muttered, "You bastard." As if a switch were thrown, a valve opened, the floodgates of Peavey's rage were thrown wide and he was awash in his hatred of Joe Pruitt.

He slammed the wheel again, and again, then with both hands, harder and harder, shouting, "Fuck you! You shithole ass-bastard son-of-a-bitch! I'll kill you! You fucked up everything!" Peavey's shouts became screams inside the car, wild and freakish. He gripped the steering wheel with both hands and yanked hard as if he were trying to tear it from the column. He rocked in his seat and the car bounced violently on its springs. "Kill you! Kill you, you bastard! Killyoukillyoukillyou!" With each shout he shoved, then yanked on the wheel.

The wave was gone as fast as it had come, and Peavey sat back in the seat, puffing hard. His chest hurt even more than a minute ago, and the pain in his head had gone from a throbbing ache to searing, knife-edged agony. He reached back and probed at the edges of the wound, his fingers coming away wet with fresh blood.

He wiped his hand on his jeans and reached out for the rifle sitting in the seat next to him, placing it on his lap. With both hands back on the wheel, Peavey glared out the window, watching down the dark highway. To the night, and the van he was certain was heading his way, he whispered, "Kill you."

Chapter 64

The rumble-strip vibrated the tires on the right side of the van and Joe corrected, bring the vehicle back into the center of the lane. The inside of his head felt like it was stuffed with wet cotton batting. Thoughts were sluggish, and it seemed to take a second or two longer for his body to respond to commands.

His muscles felt like they were thrumming with a weird vibration, as if they were being charged with a low-level current. The night outside the van didn't seem quite as dark. Morning was coming.

To Joe it seemed as if the world had taken on a strange shimmering glow around the edges. A surreal feeling, like the road and trees and dashboard, everything, weren't quite there. Objects held on the edge of reality, shifting back and forth between time and space. "So tired," he muttered as the rumble-strip vibrated again.

He jerked his head up, forced his eyes wide. Soon. Have to get there soon, he thought.

Joe glanced at the phone on the dashboard. The trip time remaining read forty minutes. He would have sworn that he checked it half-an-hour ago, and it had read forty-five minutes. Jesus, come on, he thought to himself, how long is this damn road, anyway?

Joe grabbed his bottle of water, spun the top off and took a swig, then he held the bottle out in front of his face. It was half full. He thought for a moment, grunted and shrugged, then upended the bottle over his head. The cool water felt amazing. He tossed the bottle to the floor and scrubbed at the back of his neck, then wiped his hand over his face, as if trying to rub the water and its rejuvenating effects into his skin.

He punched up the volume a little on the radio. Joe normally despised pseudo-comic morning talk-show radio programs. He found them annoying instead of entertaining. Now, they were a droning distraction from his own exhaustion. The incessant voices giving him something to focus on other than the road and his own aches and pains.

"Kimmy- sorry, Kim. Another bottle of water please?" He already had to urinate, but the water helped. Another dousing might be in order, too, he thought.

"Whadda ya know, Joe?" the girl asked with a half-smile as she passed him the plastic bottle.

Joe grinned faintly and said, "Haven't heard that one in, like, a whole day."

"At least its not Dad jokes, right?"

Joe nodded, "Yeah, I guess so."

The girl glanced at the GPS on the phone. "We really have thirty-five minutes left? Feels like we've been driving forever."

"Oh now, you and the others aren't gonna start asking if we're there yet, are you?"

The girl's smile grew a little wider. "We just might, if it'll help you stay awake."

"Right now, Kim, I'm not sure a nuclear blast would be fully effective in waking me up."

"I offered to drive."

Joe laughed softly, "Yeah. You did. It won't be much longer now."

The girl pointed at the windshield and said, "Hey, can we stop there, a couple of us need to pee."

The small station appeared dark. "Sorry, it looks like its not open yet. Besides, I really don't want to stop until we get to the FBI office in Little Rock."

He glanced down at the speedometer. "I'll go a bit faster, okay?" He pushed the van from seventy-two up to seventy-five.

"That works." The girl disappeared behind his seat once more, then popped back into view next to him. "Hey, Joe?"

"Yeah?"

"Thanks for, you know, saving us and stuff."

Joe smiled. "You're welcome, Kim."

The girl vanished, then popped back up beside him a second later.

"Hey, Joe?"

"Yes?"

"You can call me Kimmy."

Joe's smile was genuine. Painful, but genuine.

"Cool. Thanks, Kimmy."

The girl dropped back behind his seat again.

These girls had been through so much, and he doubted any of their lives would ever go back to being the same as they were before, but he hoped, prayed that they could find some semblance of normalcy. Kim was tough, but she was still a kid, and his heart broke a little for her, for each one of them, including the ones that Meryl and Malik had taken away.

Joe understood that these girls were just a small portion of the large numbers of women and girls that went missing every day, used, abused, traded and sold. Through accident or providence, he was in a position (a mostly painful one) to help these girls. So many out there would get no help. There was no rescue coming, and their fates were something far beyond the average person's comprehension.

Joe watched the sign for a second as they passed the gas station and convenience store. Will's Junction. He would have loved to stop, let everyone go to the bathroom. Even if the shop had been open, he had meant what he told Kim about stopping. "No sleep 'til Little Rock" he muttered to the windshield.

He bumped the window down a little further, drawing a deep breath of the cool air. He looked up at the rearview mirror out of habit and caught a dim glimpse of the girls huddled in the back. Soon, girls, he thought, we'll be there soon.

He caught a glimpse of light in his side mirror and looked out at the reflection. Headlights had appeared behind the van. Over the radio and the rushing of the wind, he heard tires squeal, then the ripping stutter of a machine gun.

Joe's heart seemed to drop into his stomach, then leap into his throat as bullets slammed into the back of the van.

Peavey.

Inside, his mind raced, and the only thing he could think was No-No-No, like a broken-hearted mantra. Joe pressed on the gas, but the van accelerated slowly, and Peavey was already right there on his tail.

The gun clattered again, and bullets struck the back of the van with a hard, hollow sound. The girls were screaming now, and Joe had to shout to be heard over them.

"Lay down, flat on the floor, all of you! Huddle up and stay close!"

"Joe!"

"I know Kimmy, I'm going to try to get away from him again!"

The van was up to seventy-five, then pushing eighty, rocking hard as Joe powered down the highway with a madman on his tail. His eyes flicked down to the GPS map on the phone, a small part of him wishing they had somehow magically transported and were now only seconds from the safety of the authorities.

Twenty-five miles to the FBI office. Less than thirty minutes. Maybe far sooner at this speed, but the map showed the road ahead was curvy and he knew he wouldn't be able to keep pushing so hard. He would flip the van and give Peavey exactly what he wanted.

More gunfire, bullets cracked against the side of the van, punching small holes only inches above the girls laying on the floor. Their screams filled the van and seemed to vibrate Joe's skull, as if it would shatter from the pitch like fine crystal.

Leaning with the van around a curve, Joe prayed for help and drove hard. The gun ripped another line of bullets into the van, and Joe felt someone kick his seat, and something hot and angry chewed through his back, low, and to the right. He cried out with the fresh, new pain and understood he had just taken a bullet. He only hoped that nothing vital had been hit.

He still had to get to Little Rock.

Chapter 65

Peavey had jerked to full consciousness just as the van passed in front of the idling Camaro. He had had been in a half-state of sleep and chided himself for succumbing to pain and exhaustion.

He dropped the car into gear, tromped the pedal and swerved out behind the van with a squeal of the tires, pulling the rifle into his lap the moment the car was straight.

With his left hand, he poked the gun out the side window, and triggered a burst. The rifle wasn't meant to be fired one handed, and it climbed badly, stitching bullets up the back of the van.

He needed to get alongside the van for a clear shot at Joe.

Peavey fired again, gritting his teeth at the stuttering pain inside his skull. He pulled the trigger again, firing several more rounds, and once more seconds later. The weapon clicked on an empty chamber and Peavey slowed while trying to work the gun with one hand, removing the top-loading magazine and dropping in another, jerking the charging handle to set a new round in the chamber.

The van had pulled ahead several yards.

Gotta stop wasting bullets, he thought. Get beside him and look into his damn face before I shoot him.

Peavey held the rifle in his right hand,

guiding the car with his left; he dropped the pedal to the floor once more and the heavy car shot forward. He moved to the left lane and pulled up on the van like it was standing still waiting for him. The big vehicle just couldn't compare when it came to speed or maneuverability.

A dark grin spread across Peavey's face as Joe's head came into view. The perfect target.

Chapter 66

Joe glanced at the side-mirror and saw the car suddenly drop back several yards. What the hell's he doing? Joe wondered, his thoughts frantic. Reaching down to his right side, Joe felt for a wound. The bullet was still inside, it hadn't exited. He wasn't dead, so whatever damage it had done, it wasn't immediately fatal.

In the process of feeling for the injury, Joe was reminded that he still carried the pistol in his right jacket pocket. He felt a stab of anger at himself for forgetting it was there. He tugged the pistol free and took his other hand off the wheel for a moment to check that that there was a bullet in the chamber. He couldn't remember how many rounds were in the magazine. Whether it was one or ten, it would have to be enough.

Peavey's headlights drew closer and he was now in the left lane. He's coming around. Shit. Joe willed the van to move faster, but he knew there was no way he could compete with the raw power under the car's hood.

Peavey hadn't fired again. Maybe that's why he had slowed. He was out of bullets. I can only hope, Joe thought.

Joe caught a glint of light on water and looked to his left to see the sun peeking above the horizon. He saw a sign that read Lake Maumelle and risked a glance at the GPS. Twenty miles.

As he turned to look into the side-mirror

again the Camaro pulled up beside the van, and Joe could see Peavey's wildly grinning face. To him, it was the face of death staring back.

Peavey lifted the rifle and fired, looking directly into Joe's eyes.

Joe ducked to the side and pressed the gas pedal hard. Bullets hammered the van as it surged forward, stitching down its side.

Joe felt a small, hard fist punch him in the side, under his ribs. He grunted at yet another pain, and the shock of the bullet made his head swim.

Behind him the girls shouted, then began screaming high and loud.

Joe popped back up in the seat, lifted the pistol and fired out the window. Bullets hit the hood of the car, and it backed off just enough so that Joe was unable to get another shot at it.

Glancing ahead, Joe saw two things at once, they were approaching a levy and bridge that cut across a narrow cove of the lake, and there was a car coming down the highway toward them.

He started to reach for the headlight switch, to flash the other driver, when Peavey's gun rattled again. More bullets hitting the van. The girls screaming and shouting.

The Camaro appeared at the side window again.

Too much. All too much. He had two bullets in him. He was struggling to draw a deep breath. The girls were screaming. The oncoming car. Peavey and the Camaro and the machine gun. God, please let this nightmare end. Please.

Joe stood on the gas pedal and the van rocked harder. He hit the edge of the bridge and powered forward, the approaching headlights grew closer every second, but he couldn't worry about that driver.

The headlights disappeared from the side mirror, and a moment later the car blew past, its horn blaring angrily. Through gritted teeth, Joe said, "Yeah, tell me about it, buddy."

He crossed the short portion of the bridge that actually passed over open water, and seconds later left the bridge and levy altogether. There was a long ninety-degree turn just ahead.

"Damn it!" he shouted. Joe let off the gas, and the headlights reappeared behind him, glaring in the side-mirror. The gun chattered again as Peavey pulled alongside, still wearing his that evil grin.

Joe lifted the pistol, extending his right arm across his body. He wanted nothing more at that moment, than to shoot Peavey right in the mouth, blow that stupid grin off his face.

Joe jerked the trigger, twice, three times. The gun fell empty, but Joe saw Peavey twitch. He didn't know if he had hit the kidnapper, but the Camaro backed off again and Joe focused on rounding the big curve.

He dropped the useless weapon to the floor and said, "Listen girls, the next time he's right beside me, I'm going to try to ram him. All of you, move over to the…" He had to pause to get his breath. "…to the right side of the van and stay as low as you can. Okay? Kimmy, can you make sure they get it done, like…" another breath, "…right now?"

There was no response from Kim and Joe said, "Kimmy?" Joe's heart hammered, and a spike of terror ran through his chest. "Kimmy, answer me!"

A sobbing girl said, "Mr. Joe. She's not moving. I think she's hurt."

Chapter 67

Peavey swore violently at the window, spittle spraying from his mouth, flecking the windshield. One of Joe's bullets had clipped his left bicep before burying itself in the door panel.

There had been no choice other than to let the oncoming car pass. There had been nowhere else to go and playing chicken with the car would have defeated his purpose, which now was to kill Joe. The laptop was forgotten, as were the girls. Meryl and the punishment she would deal out for everything that had happened tonight wasn't even a consideration. Joe Pruitt had to die.

"Damn it!" Peavey spat. They were approaching a long ninety-degree turn and he had to back off. There was no way he was going to try pulling alongside the van for that. He took a second to check the magazine of the FN P90. It was almost empty, and he had only one magazine left. Have to get it done soon.

As the morning grew on and the sun rose higher, more cars would be on the highway. Anthony Peavey didn't care about the other drivers at all, other than that they might impede his mission.

Peavey was aware that they were closing in on Little Rock. Maybe…twenty minutes out. The closer they got to the city, the more likely they were to be seen by another cop.

Through the fuzzy pain in his head, Peavey

wondered how any of this had happened. Was it fate? Punishment? One average nobody suddenly pulls a big hero act and now his entire operation was shot to hell. All of his men dead, as well as Aikman's crew. The girls taken from him. How ironic, he thought.

As long as he killed Joe Pruitt, nothing else really seemed to matter right then. They came out of the long curve and in seconds, the van had pushed back up to seventy miles an hour. Peavey matched it and passed that easily, the Camaro still rumbling happily along, chewing up the road in front of him.

He raised the rifle as he pulled alongside the van once more. Clenching his teeth, the muscles in his jaw standing, Peavey triggered the weapon just as the side of Joe's face came into view.

Chapter 68

Joe had to fight the absurd urge to jump into the back to check on the girl, as if he could initiate autopilot and move about freely. "Girls? Shake her! Dump some water on her! Slap her face, see if you can get her to wake up!"

He hauled on the wheel, bringing the van out of the curve. He expected Peavey to pull alongside as soon as they left it, and he wasn't disappointed. Joe tromped the gas pedal, pushing the van back to seventy as quickly as possible.

He had to focus on the road, on Peavey and whatever he was about to do next. As the lights pulled alongside him, Joe gripped the wheel hard with both hands, trying to command his body to draw slow easy breaths.

Without consciously intending to do so, Joe swerved to the right, crossing the rumble strip at the same time Peavey's weapon cracked off several shots. None of them hit the van.

Watching the road ahead, Joe could see they were coming up on another narrow bridge, this one along a short slip of levy, with the usual steel guardrail running along both sides.

He had only a few seconds to make his thought work. The Camaro pulled directly alongside, and Joe looked down then threw himself to the side, ducking down just as Peavey jabbed the rifle out in one hand and triggered he gun. Bullets tore through the air and punched up through the ceiling. They would have gone through his head if he had been half a second slower.

Sitting back up in the seat, Joe's eyes flicked forward. They were seconds from the bridge. He looked down at Peavey, raised his left hand and flipped the kidnapper his middle finger as he pulled the wheel to right, crossing the rumble strip, putting another foot of space between them. Joe heard Peavey's shout and grinned even as he jerked the wheel hard to the left.

The lumbering van slammed into the side of the Camaro, and Joe hit the gas pedal hard. The Camaro roared as if wounded, and Peavey's shout carried high. The girls in the back screamed as they were violently tossed about.

Joe kept the pressure on for another second, and the Camaro pulled away from him, to the left. Straight toward the curved steel end of the guard rail on the left side of the bridge.

Chapter 69

It felt as if the steering wheel had been ripped from his fingers when the van hit. The gun dropped from his hand as he reached for the wheel with both hands.

The Camaro swerved to the left, pulling away from the van.

The bridge was right there. Peavey shouted, wordless, an animalistic wail of rage.

The Camaro struck the end of the bridge on the right corner of the front bumper. The car seemed to stop for a second, as if considering what to do next, before momentum lifted the rear of the car up and threw it sideways.

Peavey's face slammed into the steering wheel. Shattered teeth were shot into the back of his throat, but he didn't have time to choke on them. The car spun to the side and began to flip as if moving on not one axis, but several different axes at once. The trunk of the Camaro burst open, throwing guns everywhere behind it when it hammered the ground next to the levy, then it was airborne for several seconds before dropping into Lake Maumelle with a wide, uneven splash.

Chapter 70

Joe glanced in the side mirror without stopping. He saw the car slam into the bridge and flip into the lake. He refused to stop or slow down. Even if Peavey had somehow survived that, there was no way for the man to come after him now.

It was becoming more difficult to draw a full breath, and the girls in the back were crying harder, bordering on screams. He wanted to say something to them…to Kimmy. To get a response that she was hurt but okay, to let the girls know they would soon be at the FBI office, but he just didn't have the air for it.

Joe kept the pedal down, slowing only for curves. After several minutes, shot a glance at the GPS. Fifteen miles left. Looking at the phone reminded him that he wanted to make several calls, let people know what was happening. He had planned on calling several different news stations, the local police and the FBI office he was heading toward. He wanted a show, a carnival of people waiting for him and the girls. That way no one could cover it up.

People had to know this kind of thing was happening right under their noses, in their towns and cities. People had to understand.

Joe grabbed the phone and moved the GPS app to the background. He picked one number from the list he had created earlier in the night, punched the selection and lifted it to his ear, praying that someone would even be there to answer the phone at this time of the morning.

"KATV, we're on your side," a far too cheerful female voice said.

Joe worked to get enough air to speak. "God, I hope so," he said. Joe began to explain what had happened, where he was going when the woman interrupted.

"Sir, let me get someone from the news desk."

Joe shook his head as if she could see him and regretted the movement. His vision began to swim almost instantly. "No… "he sucked in another difficult breath. "No time. Just listen."

He kept it short, explaining as much as he could with as few words as possible. "You get it?"

"Yes sir. FBI office, ten minutes, kidnapped girls."

"Good. Call an ambulance too." Joe clicked off the call without waiting for a response, brought the GPS app back up and placed the phone back inside the cradle on the dash.

"Girls?" His voice was almost a whisper and he had to try again. "Girls? How's Kimmy?"

One of the girls spoke up, "Um, I think she has a pulse, but, uh, I don't know. Her eyes are fluttery, and it looks like her chest is moving, but, we… I uh, don't know, ya know?"

"Okay, thank you."

Joe was coming into the edge of the city now, and he slowed the van as traffic began to increase, but he kept moving, weaving in and out, going around slower cars, occasionally hitting the horn and swearing as drivers cut in front of him.

Following the GPS, Joe left AR-10 and turn onto Chenal Parkway. It was about six miles to his next turn. Joe had just passed a Walmart Supercenter when a siren blared to life behind him, lights flashing in the mirror.

Joe stayed on course, keeping his speed low. The sun was coming up, and the day was beginning to brighten enough that he no longer needed the headlights. He left them on. They didn't matter. The cop behind them didn't matter. Peavey's dead or not-dead body lying in a lake miles behind them didn't matter.

Reaching the FBI office and getting these girls to safety was all that mattered.

If he were thinking clearly, he might have stopped, gotten help from the officer. He was dizzy from pain, and breathing was far too difficult. The blurred edges of his vision had seemed to grow wider. Now, the little red pip on the GPS map was his sole focus, his destination, his final mission.

Cady Lynn, sweetheart, I miss you kiddo, he thought. Daddy wants to come home.

The van swerved, and he tried to sit up straighter, pulling the wheel to get back on course. He bumped another car. The police cruiser was still wailing painfully behind him. The girls were crying, but he had no more words for them.

His turn approached, and he exited the

parkway for Kanis Road, cutting the curve too sharply, the tires scraping the curb. He over-corrected and went too far into the left lane. A horn blared, and a siren wailed and the road curved and the world was blurry, and oh he hurt and three miles was three hundred miles.

Closer now. Another siren joined the first, screaming at him to stop. Stop right now. Pull over. The van was slowing, he could feel it.

Joe clenched his teeth, hard. Pain worked its way from his jaw to his brain, and the fog cleared just a little. Joe pulled himself straighter in the seat and gripped the wheel tight.

"One mile to your destination."

"Thanks," Joe whispered to the sweet, if slightly electronic voice of the woman.

A minute later, he made a turn, then another turn, just following the little red arrow on the phone. Going where it told him to go.

There, in front of him, he saw a news van, and several men and women in jackets and ties and then they went a little blurry. There was the gate. Metal gate. Not like the one where he had squished the guy, this was a different metal gate, with FBI standing there. The FBI.

Joe's foot moved to the brake and slipped. He tried again, pulling the wheel toward the gate and the tiny guard shack behind it.

In the shapes and shadows Joe saw Peavey point a pistol at him. It didn't register that he had left Peavey far behind. He jerked the wheel at the last second.

The van crashed to a stop against a concrete

post, tearing the corner of a gate loose.

Sounds, shouting, sirens. The smell of hot engine oil. Weeping from the back of the van. The door was torn open, someone grabbed him.

As he was dragged from the van, Joe, nearly unconscious, murmured, "Help Cady… mean… Kimmy. Help… the girls." The blurry world shifted, becoming even more indistinct, and Joe Pruitt closed his eyes.

Chapter 71

Sounds were the first thing Joe recognized. Muted voices speaking, squeaking shoes, rattling wheels, a faint but incessant beeping. He thought he heard Anne's voice and opened his eyes, a moment later a blurry shape leaned over him.

"Mr. Pruitt? Joe?"

A man's voice, but he was as formless as Joe's own thoughts. Joe's eyes tracked back and forth for several seconds, then fell shut once more.

When he woke again, thinking was easier, and he was able to focus enough to realize he was in a hospital. He was attached to a monitor for his vitals, the beeping low, the volume turned down.

He moved his head by small degrees, taking in the mostly empty room. The wall-hung television, the empty chair with a coat of some kind thrown over the arm, a rolling table with some papers and a plastic water pitcher and cup sitting on it.

He tried to reach up, touch his face, run his hands over his hair. His arms jerked to a stop as soon as he tried to move them. Panic flared, and the cardiac monitor reflected it with an increased beeping. Joe pulled, struggling against the heavy straps, but he was far too weak to do little else.

A voice came from his right, a male voice. "Whoa, take it easy there Mr. Pruitt." Joe turned to look at the man who had just stepped out of what he assumed was a bathroom, wiping his hands on a towel.

Joe's lips formed words, but he found his voice weak, almost a whisper. "Who…?"

The man walked up to the bedside, placed his hands on the rail, looked down into Joe's frightened eyes and said, "Mr. Pruitt, I'm Special Agent Emmet Forney with the FBI."

Joe looked down as the tall man placed a hand on Joe's wrist, on the restraint. "You had some bad moments while you were unconscious, violent movement, kind of like you were fighting someone. The restraints were for your own protection, Mr. Pruitt. Let me get a doctor or someone to…"

The door to his room opened and a nurse walked in, another man, about five-feet eight with brown hair. He looked at Joe, then spoke to the agent. "I've let the doctor know he's awake, agent, she'll be here shortly."

"I was just getting ready to call for someone, thanks."

The nurse walked over to Joe, checked his vital signs on the monitor, made notations on a chart and said, somewhat sheepishly, "It's an honor Sir, I would shake your hand, but…" he nodded toward Joe's restraints.

Joe's brow pulled together in confusion.

The nurse said, "The doctor will be here in just a moment. Then we can probably take those off, okay? I'm Kevin, by the way. If you need anything, just hit the red button." Kevin placed a call unit into Joe's left hand.

Everyone turned when a voice from the door said, "Mr. Pruitt, I'm glad to see you're awake." The woman strode into the room as if she owned it, her back straight, head high. Her white lab-coat was in stark contrast to her dark brown skin. The woman seemed to smile with her eyes as well as her mouth. She stepped up beside Agent Forney, looked down at Joe and said, "I'm Doctor Cynthia Carlin, Mr. Pruitt, I've been seeing to your care since you've been here at Baptist Health Medical Center."

Joe looked around the bed at all the faces smiling at him. He still felt fuzzy, not fully awake. His voice was slightly stronger than a moment before, but it still came out like a forced whisper. "Everyone keeps calling me "Mr. Pruitt." I'm just Joe."

All three of the people in the room laughed and smiled. The Agent sat down in the chair and waited while Kevin released the restraints and the Doctor explained to him the severity of his wounds. Multiple scrapes and bruising, the fractured, swollen jaw, damage to his right kidney and the punctured left lung and more.

"Frankly, Mr. Pruitt, sorry... Joe, you nearly died. It's a wonder you survived."

Joe looked up at the doctor, then around at Kevin and the Agent. To the doctor he asked, "How long? How long have I been here?"

The woman's tone lowered, "You've been here four days, Joe. Your surgeries went well, but we thought it best to simply let your body do what it needed to do."

Joe looked down the bed, around the room, his face tight. "Four days? What about... what about the girls? Are they okay? Kimmy was hurt. Is she here too?"

Joe saw the Doctor glance at the agent before she said, "Sorry Joe, I don't really have any information on the girls. I'll leave you and Agent Forney to talk, and I'll come back in a little while. If you need anything, please, just hit the button."

The doctor left, followed closely by Kevin, who shot a quick glance back over his shoulder and gave Joe a sad, knowing smile.

Agent Forney sat forward in the chair, on it's edge, and leaned toward Joe. "Before you ask me anything, I want you to know, the girls have told us everything that happened, Joe. At least everything they know. You're a hero, Mr. Pruitt. They themselves will tell you that."

Joe swallowed hard and asked, "What about Kim? They said she was hurt, shot, in the van. I couldn't stop. Is she okay? What...?"

Agent Forney looked down at the floor, at his hands, then back up and Joe felt his direct gaze. "Kim's injuries were... fatal, Mr. Pruitt. She had been laying on the floor of the van, her arms around another girl, shielding her. The bullet entered her back and struck her heart. Her death was nearly instantaneous."

The room seemed to spin away as that familiar, uncomfortable knot formed in Joe's throat. It was surreal, and it hurt. Joe lifted his hands to his face as if to hide, and he felt the first hot tears on his palms. His body shook as the sobs came, harder and harder. Joe Pruitt wept openly for Kim, and for all the lost little girls he couldn't save.

Joe felt a hand on his arm, and Agent Forney's voice was gentle when he said, "I'm sorry."

Joe grabbed the hand, held it, clasping it like it was the only thing anchoring him to the world and Forney sat there until Joe's tears stopped.

Joe finally released the agent's hand, and the two men sat in silence for a while. Eventually, Joe looked at the FBI agent, directly into the man's eyes and said, "I'm sorry."

"It's fine. Everyone's allowed some tears, especially after what you went through."

"No, I mean, about…"

The agents gaze was direct and unwavering. "I know, Mr. Pruitt."

Joe held the man's eyes for several heartbeats and nodded. He drew a breath, thankful that he was able to do so, and let it out slowly, a protracted sigh. "Agent Forney, please don't call me "Mr. Pruitt" anymore, okay?"

The man pursed his lips and nodded. "You got it, Joe. There are some things I want to talk to you about. Before I do, however, I want you see something."

Forney lifted the hand unit from the bed and pressed the button for the TV across the room. The screen flickered to life and the agent spun the little wheel on the side to bring up the tinny volume of the small speaker. It was already tuned to a news station.

"It won't really make anything better, but it might help you, well, process everything that's happened."

Joe nodded and watched.

Chapter 72

"The apparent suicide of New York Senator Dorian Wilkins yesterday has caused ripples across Capitol Hill and the nation. Senator Wilkins, best known for his shouting matches with fellow politicians on both sides of the aisle, as well as his heavily pro-union stance, will be missed by many. His wife and three daughters are asking for privacy during this difficult time."

Joe turned from the TV to look at Agent Forney. "The man had three daughters. How could someone..." Joe trailed off for a moment.

Agent Forney said, "Evil hearts, sick people, they come in all forms, Joe. I've seen it more than I care to admit."

Joe turned the volume down and glared at the television as it cut to a commercial. "So, this bastard offs himself and now he's just going to get away with it? He'll get accolades and memorials, and no one will ever know what he was involved in?"

"I'm not sure it'll work like that this time around, Joe. Not in this case. Keep watching, then we'll talk."

Joe cocked his head at an angle as the Agent spoke and realized that the man's words sounded like they were coming through a filter in his left ear, as if it were packed with a bit of cotton. He rubbed at it for a moment, then turned up the volume on the hand-unit once more. After listening for several seconds, he was certain that there was something wrong with his hearing in that ear. He would have to tell the doctor.

The anchor was saying, … *"girls are now back with their families after this harrowing ordeal. We have Lindsey Enspaugh, with her parents and Dana Richards and her mom with us this morning. Good morning, thank you for joining us."*

As they all returned their greetings, Joe recognized Lindsey's voice as the one that had told him Kim was hurt. Dana was the girl Joe had first seen taken on the street.

He listened while the girls described what they were doing, where they had been when they were kidnapped. How they had been treated by their kidnappers, and what little they knew of their intentions with the girls.

"We, uh, heard fighting, and gunshots and stuff. Then Joe was there. He let us all go, where we were chained up on the beds and got us water. Then he left for a while, said he had to get stuff ready for us to leave, explained that we were going to the FBI. Kim had gone out to look for him, and then she came back a few minutes later and told us that he had a van and we were going to leave."

"Now, that would be Kim Oberfield, correct?"

"Uh, yeah. She was the one that got, you know, shot." The girl's face began to tighten as Joe watched, tears forming in her eyes, her bottom lip trembling. Dana was also tearing up as Lindsey spoke.

"Lindsey, Dana, if you could say anything to Joe right now, what would tell him?"

Both girls looked directly into the camera and Lindsey said. "Thank you, Joe, for rescuing us. I hope you're okay." Dana echoed Lindsey's comments.

"Would you say Joe is a hero?"

Both girls said, *"Yeah, for sure."* Their parents were nodding emphatically beside them.

"Thank you, girls, for visiting with us today. I know this hasn't been easy for any of you." The anchor turned toward the camera and said, *"The man being hailed the hero, and called "Average Joe" Pruitt, a window-glass repairman from southern Missouri. Who is he? More on Joe Pruitt when we return."*

Joe clicked the TV off. "I'm no hero," he said as if speaking to the television. He turned to look at the Agent. "I'm not a hero."

Agent Forney nodded toward the T.V. *"They* say you are."

"Well, I'm not."

"Joe, because of that laptop we found in the van, and the girl's testimonies, a lot of people are going down for this. There are connections that range worldwide, from the Middle-East, to Rome and Britain, and, well, just about everywhere it seems. This Anthony Peavey guy must have been majorly paranoid about someone screwing him over, because he had files on every person he had ever worked with."

"Can you use it, to, you know, catch some of them? Put them away?"

"We've already begun, Joe. And there are people involved in the investigation that want to make sure that Senator Wilkins is held accountable, even if it's posthumously."

Joe nodded, his brow knitted in thought.

"There are a few things I want to clarify with you, Joe. But there are some things I want you to understand first."

"Yeah, okay."

"You're the hero of the week. The next big thing will come along, people will move on, you'll be forgotten about, mostly. But, there are some who don't forget, ever. Because of what you've done, there are a lot of people going to prison, political careers ruined, fortunes lost. Some people, well, they might want retribution for that. I'm not saying it'll happen, Joe, but it's something I want to make sure you're aware of. Most of these people are running, trying to go underground, or spending the hell out of some money just to try to keep their names out of the papers and off the TV."

Joe nodded, acknowledging the Agent and what he was saying. "I understand. Watch my back and all that."

"Yeah, watch your back. This isn't going to be anything like the movies, Joe. No riding off into the sunset the hero. There will be inquests and investigations. You're going to be doing some testifying and may even have to account for you own actions, and all the deaths you caused during this event. The next few months could be a challenge. I just want you to be fully aware."

"Agent Forney, will I be placed under arrest?"

The Agent shook his head. "No, as far as we're concerned, you're a good guy, Joe, and there are no plans to bring any charges against you, though there's always an asshole or two who think guys like you shouldn't have fought so hard, killed so many in the defense of others."

"Thank you," Joe said. He rested his head back on the pillow, and could feel gravity pulling at his eyes, trying to close them again.

"Joe, you're tired, and there's plenty of time to talk. You get some rest, and I'll come back soon." Agent Forney stood, slung his coat on, and shook Joe's hand. "You might not think so, but, you really are a hero, Joe Pruitt. And there's not a damn thing *average* about you."

Joe watched as Forney walked away, staring at the door for a long moment after if closed. "Hero." He said the word aloud, as if tasting it. To Joe, the word was bitter and felt strange on his tongue.

Hero.

Epilogue

Joe lowered himself slowly into a chair on the front porch of his house and watched the cars drive by for several minutes. In his fingers he held a long white envelope, which he tapped unconsciously against his leg as he looked out over his tiny lawn, and to the street beyond.

Occasionally, he would see a news-van creep by, or lookie-loos craning their necks to get a view of the house, and the hero inside, though even that had tapered off over the past couple of weeks.

Forney had been right, time moved on. The next big newsworthy thing happened, and Joe was forgotten about, mostly. He was glad. Joe wasn't sure if life would ever return to normal, but he wished for that sense of normalcy. Go to work, come home, watch TV, drink a beer.

He checked his watch. 11:30. Paulie would be showing up soon to help him pack and get the house ready for potential buyers. Once the house was clean and empty of Joe's personal belongings, the agent wanted to come by to take pictures for the listing.

Joe sat forward in the chair and looked down at the envelope. He turned it in his hands and flipped it over several times. Tapped it against his fingers and moved to open it before shuffling it around once more.

He was afraid to see what was inside.

In the corner, where the return address

usually was, there was only a last name. Oberfield.

Joe checked his watch again. 11:32.

Just open it, Joe, he chided himself.

He pinched a corner of the envelope to tear it away and the new phone clipped to his belt rang. He glanced at the screen before answering. Anne's number.

"Hello?"

"Hi, Daddy!"

"Hey, kiddo! Wasn't expecting you to call. How are you doing?"

"I'm good. Mom's making grilled cheese for lunch."

"Mmm, grilled cheese. Nothing quite so good as grilled cheese, right?"

"Yep, that's what I always say. Hey Daddy, when are you going to be here?"

"Pretty soon, kiddo. Uncle Paulie's on his way over to help me finish packing, then, I have to meet with a real-estate agent and take care of some things with him. It'll take me a few more days to get everything all lined out, then I'm headed your way."

"Awesome! There's lots of fun stuff to do around here. I wanna show you this amusement park. It's so much fun!"

Joe smiled at his daughter's infectious happiness. "That sounds like a date, Cady Lynn. I can't wait."

"Me either, Dad. Get here soon! The grilled cheeses are done, gotta go. Mom says Hi."

"Hi back to mom. See you soon,

sweetheart."

"Bye, Dad."

"Bye."

Joe tapped the screen and the call went silent. Seconds later, the screen went dark and he placed the phone beside him on a small, round glass-topped outdoor table.

The envelope was thin. He tore it open carefully and tipped out the contents. A note, wrapped around a photograph.

The note was brief and bittersweet, and he would keep the words to himself. They were meant for him, and him alone.

The picture of Kim Oberfield was small, probably her last school photo, wallet-sized, which is where he placed it after whispering "I'm sorry." That he had been unable save her along with the others would always hurt, like the ache in his jaw, persistent, occasionally sharp, but always there.

Joe stood and turned to walk inside the house when a horn blared from the street, and Paulie's battered old pickup bumped up into his narrow driveway. Joe swiped at his eyes and walked down the steps, greeting his old friend with a hug.

"You okay, buddy?"

Joe nodded. "I will be. Cady Lynn just called. She's getting excited."

Paulie smiled, clapped him on the back and said, "Well, we can't keep your daughter waiting, man. Let's get you moved to California."

END

ABOUT THE AUTHOR

I write things. I've been doing it for a really long time, but only recently did I start publishing. Soon after that I was lucky enough to land a job as the editorial assistant for a small newspaper. Now someone actually pays me to write, which is pretty cool. Other than that, I have no credentials to speak of, no education worth noting. I haven't done anything amazing like single-handedly save an entire tribe of Ugandan children from Ebola or serve overseas and save my entire squad from a tribe of Ugandan children with Ebola.

Along with the independently published American Revenant zombie apocalypse series set in and around Hannibal, Missouri I dabble in horror and science-fiction, mostly in short stories, as well as the occasional thriller. I've also written several short screenplays with plans to eventually script a feature-length film.

Made in the USA
Columbia, SC
08 February 2025

52884259R00170